APPALACHIAN
LOVE STORIES

❧❧

A gift to

_____

from

_____

_____, 20_____

❧❧

Illustrations by
JIM MARSH

APPALACHIAN LOVE STORIES

Compiled and Edited by

James M. Gifford
Edwina Pendarvis

Jesse Stuart Foundation
Ashland, Kentucky
2001

Dedicated to every reader
who finds a little bit of his/her life
in the pages of this book.

FIRST EDITION

3 2530 60552 8791

Library of Congress Cataloging-in-Publication Data

Appalachian love stories/compiled and edited by Edwina Pendarvis, James M. Gifford.
    p.cm.
    ISBN 0-945084-89-7
    1. Love stories, American--Appalachian Region, Southern. 2. Appalachian Region,
Southern--Fiction. I. Pendarvis, Edwina D. II. Gifford, James M.

PS554 .A3 2001
813'.085083276--dc21   2001016024

813.085083276
APPA

Illustrations by Jim Marsh

Published by:
Jesse Stuart Foundation
1645 Winchester Avenue
P.O. Box 669
Ashland, KY 41105
(606) 326-1667

CONTENTS

INTRODUCTION

Several years ago the Jesse Stuart Foundation published a theme book entitled *Appalachian Christmas Stories*. The book was the best seller at the 1998 Kentucky Book Fair, and it was well received by reviewers and popular with general public readers. So we decided to do a series of companion books with universal themes; our first is *Appalachian Love Stories*. We cast a broad net for material in order to include some "new authors," along with established greats like Jesse Stuart and Billy C. Clark. We solicited submissions from Jesse Stuart Foundation Board Members and, in the Foundation's newsletter, from more than 5000 Associate Members nationwide. The overwhelming response generated so many good stories that we decided to shape two books: one that focused on romantic love and another that focused on love of friends and family.

This overwhelming response was a pleasant surprise to us because when we asked our friends to name famous couples from Appalachian literature and history, about the only names anyone came up with were Johnse Hatfield and Roseanna McCoy, Li'l Abner and Daisy Mae, and Mammy and Pappy Yokum. Someone also mentioned John Henry and his pretty wife, Polly. Such a paucity of names reinforced our belief that Appalachians just aren't known for their romantic nature. No Romeo and Juliette, no Tristan and Isolde. We don't even have a Bonnie and Clyde!

And the couples people came up with don't inspire much confidence in Appalachian romance. Only Li'l Abner and Daisy Mae stayed perpetually smitten with each other. Johnse refused to marry Roseanna, Mammy bossed Pappy, and John

Henry, on his death-bed, asked Polly to take up a sledge hammer and follow in his doomed footsteps! Completing this unpromising picture of Appalachian romance are the many depictions of lazy, "do-less" husbands and long suffering, unattractive wives. No wonder people don't associate Appalachians with romance—images of Appalachian couples veer from comic to downright dour.

Reading the stories in this collection, we're struck by how much these Appalachian love stories are like other love stories. They draw on an ideal of romantic love that has been around since the late Middle Ages—the notion that true love is a life-long bond of passion between two people who are uniquely suited for each other. Some of the stories in this collection replay that old notion. Other stories play off that notion by showing exceptions to the ideal, or at least, circuitous routes to it.

Some familiar Appalachian themes are interwoven with the theme of romantic love: love of nature, interest in the past, closeness of family. No doubt this is due in part to the editorial process of calling for Appalachian love stories, and it may have as much to do with the authors' conceptions of what constitutes an Appalachian story as it has to do with the reality of Appalachia.

Most of the stories are set in central Appalachia—eastern Kentucky, eastern Tennessee, southern Ohio, and West Virginia—because the authors are mostly from there. That we didn't set any stories in southern or northern Appalachia doesn't mean we think those folks are unromantic. We just didn't get any stories from the northern or southern environs.

Because of the number of stories in this collection, we clustered the stories thematically in the table of contents.

These thematic labels are intended to give readers a hint of what the stories are about and which stories fit most closely together. We borrowed common terms, such as "in country," to designate modern war-related stories, and terms from Appalachian literature, such as Jesse Stuart's "blue dreamers," for stories about people who lived before the twentieth century, and "coal quilt," to label our two stories drawn from life in coal camps.

On the whole, these are rural stories in which the natural environment plays a large part. Most of the plot events take place outside, if not in a field or forest, then on a front porch. And most of the characters in these stories are actively engaged with the natural environment, whether they're digging ginseng, swimming, or riding horses. When they're not outside, they're likely to be at the wheel of a car or playing on a basketball court. Wherever they are, they're physically active, motivated, energetic people. The men and women in this collection form a striking contrast to the low-energy caricatures who represent Appalachians in many books and movies.

Not surprisingly, country music figures prominently in some of the stories. One story features a fiddle, and songs are heard over the radio in three other stories. Appalachian ideas about love find their most popular expression in music, which both inspires and represents conventional Appalachian romance.

The stories in this book depict the Appalachian experience from our pioneer beginnings to the Vietnam War and beyond. Many are set in the past—as far back as the French and Indian War—and almost all of them reflect a strong awareness of the importance of the past, especially the lingering effects of war. Like many Appalachian writers, these authors write about the past as a way of acknowledging history at work in their lives today and as a way of paying tribute to their forbearers, maybe too as a way of recouping losses that Appalachians have felt ever since the industrialization of the region.

Another familiar Appalachian theme that makes an appearance here is the importance of family. These stories emphasize the role of mothers, fathers, sisters, brothers, even sons and daughters, in influencing the course of romance. A related theme, but one that was something of a surprise to us, is the strong theme of love growing out of shared hardships. Sometimes this theme is expressed in a traditional fashion and harks back to the conventional romantic ideal of life-long devotion, but two of the stories feature couples who marry for practical reasons, then end up in love after all, because of the hard work they do together.

In sociological literature, Appalachian couples are often described as conforming more to conventional gender stereotypes than couples elsewhere. Maybe that's true, maybe it's not. Like Bob Snyder, the late poet, muckraker, and staunch defender of Appalachian values, we're suspicious of any general consensus about Appalachia. And, of course, we hope this collection serves as a partial corrective to scholarly speculation and popular sentiment regarding Appalachians as unlikely candidates for modern romance. We have to admit there is sexism in these stories, in part because they're set in the past. But there's an egalitarian spirit in them, too. The women in these stories are as smart, hardworking, and courageous—sometimes as reckless—as the men.

Several Jesse Stuart Foundation employees made significant contributions to this book. Rachel Minton skillfully typed the manuscript and accurately revised the disk many, many times during two-years of editing. Eleanor Kersey and Caroline Wilson helped with the proofreading. Brett Nance designed the pages and made them camera-ready. Finally, the greatest contribution to this book, beyond the work done by the authors, was made by our senior illustrator and book designer, Jim Marsh. Jim's evocative illustrations are carefully-studied and accurate in detail, and they breathe life into the pages of this book.

The Jesse Stuart Foundation is proud to present this book to the reading public. *Appalachian Love Stories* will provide hours of enjoyment for any reader, but we believe it will be especially satisfying to the people of Appalachia who may revisit parts of their own lives, loves, and courtships in this collection of stories.

James M. Gifford
Edwina Pendarvis

THE SLIPOVER SWEATER
by Jesse Stuart

"Now if you don't get the sweater," Grace said as she followed me up the narrow mountain path, "you mustn't feel
too bad. Everybody in Gadsen High School knows that you've
made your letters. Just because you don't wear them like the
other boys…."

Grace stopped walking before she finished the last sentence. And I knew why. But I didn't say anything—not right
then. I stopped a minute to look down over the cliffs into the
gorge where the mountain water swirled over the rocks, singing a melancholy song without words. Grace walked over
and stood beside me. And I knew the sound of the roaring
water did the same thing to her that it did to me. We stood
there watching this clear blue mountain water hit and swirl
over the giant water-beaten rocks, splashing into spray as it
had done for hundreds of years before we were born.

The large yellow-gold leaves sifted slowly down from
the tall poplars. And the leaves fell like big, soft, red rain-
drops from low bushy-topped sourwoods to ferny ground.
Dark frostbitten oak leaves dropped onto Grace's ripe-wheat-
colored hair. And a big yellow-gold poplar leaf fell and stuck
to my shirt. They were a little damp, for they fell from a

canopy of leaves where there was no sun.

Gold poplar leaves would look good in Jo-Anne Burton's chestnut-colored hair, I thought. And how pretty the dark oak leaves would look on her blouse. I was sorry she wasn't with me instead of Grace. I could just see Jo-Anne standing with me instead of Grace. I could just see Jo-Anne standing there with the red and yellow leaves falling on her.

I would say, "Gee, you look wonderful with those golden leaves in your dark hair."

"Do you think so?" she would answer. And I could imagine her smile and her even white teeth. She was always gay and laughing.

I didn't say anything to Grace but Grace knew how I felt about Jo-Anne. Grace and I had gone to Plum Grove grade school together for eight years. I had carried her books from the time I could remember. And then we started walking five miles across the mountains to Gadsen High School together. When we started Gadsen I was still carrying her books. I'd carried them down and up this mountain for three years. But I was not carrying her books this year and I wouldn't be again, for Gadsen was a bigger school than Plum Grove and there were many more girls. But there was only one for me and Grace knew who she was. She was the prettiest and the most popular girl in Gadsen High School. When she was a sophomore she was elected May Queen.

Grace knew why I wanted the slipover sweater. It wasn't just to show the letters and the three stripes on the sleeve I'd won playing football three years for the Gadsen Tigers. Grace knew that Roy Tomlinson had a slipover sweater and that he was trying to beat my time with Jo-Anne Burton. Grace had heard about Jo-Anne asking me one day why I didn't get a sweater.

"You've got a small waist and broad shoulders," Jo-Anne had said, "and you'd look wonderful in a slipover sweater!"

I didn't care about having a sweater until Jo-Anne had said this to me. Now I wanted it more than anything on earth. I wanted a good one, of the style, color, and brand the other boys had bought. Then I could have my G and the three stripes sewed on, as my teammates had done. They let their favorite girls wear their sweaters. Jo-Anne was wearing Roy Tomlinson's, and that hurt me.

Grace probably knew I was thinking of Jo-Anne now. And as she stood beside me, with the leaves falling onto her dress, I couldn't keep from thinking how they would look on Jo-Anne.

Why we had stopped at this high place every morning and evening for three years, I didn't know. But it was from here on the coldest days in winter, when the gorge below was a mass of ice, that we listened to the water singing its lonesome song beneath the ice. And here in early April we watched spring come back to the mountains.

We knew which trees leafed first. And even before the leaves came back we found trailing arbutus that had sprung up beside the cliffs and bloomed. Then came the percoon that sprang from the loamy coves where old logs had lain and rotted. It was the prettiest of all wildwood flowers and its season was short. Grace and I had taken bouquets of this to our high-school teachers before a sprig of green had come to the town below.

Grace shook the multicolored leaves from her hair and dress when we silently turned to move away. And I brushed the leaves from my shirt sleeves and trousers. We started up the mountain as we had done for the past three years—only I used to take Grace's arm. Now I walked in front and led the way. If there was a snake across the path, I took care of him. I just protected Grace as any boy would protect a girl he had once loved but had ceased to love since he had found another girl who meant more to him than anyone else in the world.

"If I had the money," Grace said after our long silence, "I'd let you have it, Shan, to buy your sweater."

"I'll get the money some way," I said.

Not another word was spoken while we climbed toward the ridge. But I did a lot of thinking. I was trying to figure out how I could buy that sweater. I was not going to hunt and trap wild animals any more and sell their skins just to get clothing for my own skin. Books had changed me since I'd gone to high school. I'd never have the teacher send me home because I had polecat scent on me. I'd always bought my schoolbooks and my clothes by hunting and trapping. But I'd not done it this year and I'd not do it again. I was determined about that. Books had made me want to do something in life—for my girl. And I knew now that I wanted to be a schoolteacher and teach math in Gadsen High School. And that's what I'd do.

When Grace started from the path across to her home, a big double-log house on Seaton Ridge, she said good-by. And I said good-by to her. These were the only words spoken. We used to linger a long time at this spot by a big oak tree. I looked over at the heart cut in the bark of the oak. Her initials and mine were cut side by side inside the heart. Now, if I'd had my knife, I would have gone over and shaved these initials and the heart from the oak bark. Now I hoped that she would find some boy she could love as much as I loved Jo-Anne.

When I first realized I had to get that sweater for Jo-

Anne, I had thought about asking Pa for ten dollars. But I knew he wouldn't have it, for he raised light burley tobacco, like Grace's father, and it hadn't been a good season. Pa had not made enough to buy winter clothes for my four brothers and six sisters. And another thing, I'd never in my life asked him for money. I'd made my own way. I'd told my father I'd do this if he'd only let me go to high school. He wasn't much on education. But he agreed to this and I'd stick to my end of the bargain.

That night I thought about the people I knew. I wondered if I could borrow from one of them. I didn't like to borrow, but I'd do anything to get Jo-Anne to take off Roy Tomlinson's sweater and to put mine on in place of it. Most of the people I knew did not have the money, though.

At noon the next day the idea came to me: what are banks for? Their job is to lend money to needy people—and that's why I walked straight to the Citizens' State Bank at lunch time. I was a citizen, a student at Gadsen High School, and I needed money to buy a sweater. If Mr. Cole asked me why I needed the money, I'd just tell him I wanted very much to buy myself a sweater so I could put my school letter on it and my three stripes—and be like the other high-school boys. I wouldn't mention Jo-Anne.

I stood nervously at the window. Mr. Cole was a big heavy man with blue eyes and a pleasant smile. "Something I can do for you?" he asked politely.

"Yes, sir," I stammered. "I'd like to have ten dollars."

"You want to borrow it?" he asked.

"Yes, sir." Now the worst was over and my voice was calmer.

"You go to high school, don't you?"

"Yes, sir."

"Thought I'd seen you around here," he said. "You're the star player on the Gadsen Tigers—you're Mick Stringer's boy."

"Yes, sir," I said.

"What's your first name?" He started making out a note for me.

"Shan," I said, "Shan Stringer."

He shoved the note forward for me to sign. And he didn't ask for anyone to go my security. If he had, I don't know who I could have got to sign. I wasn't old enough to borrow money at the bank. But it just seemed to me as if Mr. Cole read my mind. He knew I wanted the money badly. So he gave me nine dollars and seventy-five cents and took a quarter for interest.

"This note will be due in three months," he said. "This is October twenty-eighth. Come back January twenty-eighth. And if you can't pay it then, I'll let you renew for another three months. And then we'll expect all or partial payment.

"Thank you, Mr. Cole."

I hurried to Womack Brothers' store and bought the sweater. It had a red body with white sleeves—the Gadsen High colors. I would have Mom sew the white G on the front and the red stripes on the sleeves as soon as I got home. I was the happiest boy in the world. Gadsen High School had always been a fine place but now it was wonderful. I loved everybody but I worshiped Jo-Anne Burton.

That afternoon when Grace and I walked through the town and came to the mountain path, we talked more than we had in a long time. But I didn't mention what was in the package I was carrying. We stopped at our place on the cliffs and looked down at the swirling waters in the gorge. The dashing water did not sound melancholy to me. It was swift dance

music like a reel from old Scotland. Even the trees above us
with their arms interlaced were in love. All the world was in
love because I had got what I wanted and I was in love.

The next morning Grace was waiting for me beside the
old oak where we had cut our initials. Grace was all right, I
thought. She was almost sure to be valedictorian of our class
and she was good-looking too. But she didn't have the kind
of beauty Jo-Anne had. Jo-Anne was not only beautiful—
she was always happy, laughing and showing her pretty teeth.
She wasn't one of the best students in the class—her grades
were not high at all. But she was friendly with everybody and
as free as the wind. Her clothes were always pretty, and they
fitted her much better than Grace's did. I loved the way she
wore her clothes. I loved everything about Jo-Anne. She held
my love as firmly as the mountain loam held the roots of the
wild flowers and the big trees.

"Why are you taking that bundle back to school?" Grace
asked.

"Oh, just to be carrying something," I said.

Grace laughed as though she thought I was very funny.

We got to school early. When I had a chance to speak to
Jo-Anne alone, I told her what I had.

"Oh, Shan!" she exclaimed. "Oh, you're a darling!"

"Brand-new," I said. "You'll like it, Jo-Anne."

"Oh, I know I'll love it," she said. "I'll put it right on!"

I handed her the package and she hurried off. I was never
happier in my life. When she came back she was smiling at
me, her eyes dancing. She walked over to Roy Tomlinson
and handed a package to him. Everybody standing around was
looking at Jo-Anne in the new sweater with the three stripes
on the sleeve—the only sweater in school with three stripes.

Was Jo-Anne proud! And I was proud!

"Do you like it on me?" she asked as she walked up to me.

"Do I like it?" I said. "I love it."

She smiled happily and I was glad that Roy could see now that I was the one Jo-Anne loved. And everybody knew now that I was in love with her. Roy would probably wonder, I was thinking, how I was able to buy that sweater. He had probably thought that he would be able to keep Jo-Anne with this sweater and his two stripes because I'd never be able to buy one for her. But Roy would never know how I got it— that would be a secret between Mr. Cole, the banker, and me.

While the girls were admiring the sweater and many of my teammates were looking on, I glanced over at Roy. He stood by not saying a word, just looking at the sweater that had replaced his. I hadn't expected him to react this way, but in a few minutes Grace came in and she was wearing Roy Tomlinson's sweater.

"Boy!" Jim Darby exclaimed. "Look at Grace! Doesn't that sweater look swell on her!"

"She isn't the same girl!" Ed Patton said.

I stared at Grace. I didn't realize a sweater could make such a difference. Her clothes had never become her. But this sweater did! There were many whispers and a lot of excitement as we flocked into the auditorium. I was watching Grace move through the crowd in her new sweater when Jo-Anne edged over closer to me.

"You do like this sweater on me, don't you, Shan?" she asked.

"Sure do, Jo-Anne," I said. And I walked proudly beside her into the auditorium.

That afternoon after I had said good-by to Jo-Anne I looked around for Grace. She was just saying her good-by to Roy. When she turned toward me I could see that she was as proud of that sweater as she could be. And Roy stood there looking after us as we started toward the mountain together.

We stopped at the gorge but we didn't stay long. Grace did most of the talking and I did the listening but I didn't hear everything she said. I was wild with joy for I was thinking about Jo-Anne wearing my new red sweater.

At every football game Jo-Anne sat on the front bleachers and yelled for me. And Grace yelled for Roy Tomlinson. Once when I made an eighty-five-yard run for a touchdown Jo-Anne came up to me after the game and kissed me. I could outkick, outpass, and outrun Roy Tomlinson. And I didn't brag when I said it. He earned another stripe that season and so did I. Grace sewed Roy's third stripe on his sweater with pride. She kept the sweater clean as a pin. I'll have to admit she kept it cleaner than Jo-Anne kept mine.

When Grace was almost sure to be valedictorian, Roy Tomlinson could hardly stand the idea of our walking over the mountain together. He walked with us to the edge of Gadsen. But he never climbed the mountain and looked down at the gorge. He could just as well have come along. His going with her didn't bother me, not exactly. She did, of course, seem close to me—like a sister. As we walked along together I saw the trees along the ridge where we had our playhouse and grapevine swings. I saw the coves where we had gathered bouquets of trailing arbutus and percoon. And those initials on the oak reminded me of the days when we were little.

It was the basketball season, just before the regional tournament, when I received a notice from the bank that my note was due. With the other little expenses I had at school even twenty-five cents wasn't easy to get.

If the interest is hard to get, I thought, what will I do about the principal? What if I have to take the sweater from Jo-Anne and sell it to make a payment on the principal?

But when my mother let me have fifty cents and I paid the interest I felt much better and didn't think about it again during the basketball season. Jo-Anne came to every game and she was always urging everybody else to come. She was as proud of me and the way I played as I was proud of her and the way she looked in my sweater.

Grace was never so talkative and gay and popular as Jo-Anne and I was always glad to hear anyone pay Grace compliments. I heard Harley Potters say one day, "You know, Grace Hinton is a beautiful girl. Think, she comes five miles to school and five miles home and makes the highest grades in her class. There's something to a girl that would go through all kinds of weather and do that."

I thought so too. All through the winters when snow was on the ground and the winds blew harshly on the mountain, she and I walked back and forth to school. I walked in front and broke the path through new fallen snow. I had done that even when we went to Plum Grove. We had walked through rain and sleet together and I couldn't remember a day that she had not been good-natured. And I knew she had the durability and the toughness of a storm battered mountain oak. I didn't believe there was another girl in Gadsen High School who could have done what Grace had done. And now to the Gadsen boys and girls she was as pretty as a cove sapling. Yet I was sure I would never go back to Grace. I'd always love Jo-Anne.

I only hoped that Roy Tomlinson appreciated Grace. I got tired of looking at his sweater so often. Sometimes I

wondered if I were jealous of him for making his third stripe.
But I was sure I wasn't because I had four, and I had the most
popular and beautiful girl in the world. I decided I was tired
of looking at it just because Grace never wore anything else.
I could hardly remember what Grace's clothes had looked
like before.

When the heavy snows of January and February passed
away in melted snow and ran down the gorge in deep foam-
ing waters, I grew as melancholy as the song of this swollen
little winter river. Jo-Anne didn't know what was worrying
me. Sometimes I wished she would ask but she never did.
And that hurt me too. If I didn't always smile at something
she said, she acted impatient with me. I'm sure I could not
have told her about the note due in April, if she had asked.
But I looked for some kind of sympathy because I thought
I needed it and that she loved me so much she would want
to cheer me up. Instead, she kept asking me if I didn't love
her and if I did, why didn't I show it the way all the other
boys did?

So I tried my best to cheer up. I didn't want to lose her
but I did have to figure out some way to make money. I
couldn't hunt now even if I'd change my mind about kill-
ing animals. Spring was on the way and animal pelts weren't
good now.

One day Grace said to me, "What is the matter with you,
Shan?" That was in late March as we were watching the blue
melted snow waters roll down the gorge where the white
dogwood sprays bent down to touch them. "I know something is bothering you."

"No it isn't," I said, "I'm all right."

"If I can ever help you, I'll be glad to," she said. "Just let
me know."

Her words made me feel better. I didn't want to tell her that I'd never been in debt before and that a debt worried me to death. So I didn't say anything.

After the snow had melted from the mountain, I grew more despondent. Neither the sight of Jo-Anne nor of Grace could cheer me. My grades went down and some of the teachers asked me what had happened to me. Everyone around me seemed happy, for April had come again. And Jo-Anne seemed gayer than ever. Several of my teammates had their eyes on her constantly and it only made me more despondent.

Grace coaxed me again one day to tell her what was wrong. "You always like spring on the mountain," she said.

Then I decided I had to tell somebody my trouble and she was the one to tell. "Grace," I confessed, "I need money—ten dollars!"

"I don't have it," Grace said quietly. "If I did, you could have it. But that doesn't help. Maybe I'll think of a way...."

I didn't think she would, but it made me feel better—just to share my worry.

On April fifteenth something happened to me that the whole school witnessed. We were gathering for assembly period when Jo-Anne handed my sweater back to me!

"I'm tired of it," she said, without her pretty smile on her lips. "And I'm tired of your ways. You go around with your lower lip drooped as if the world had turned upside down and smashed you. You never have anything to say. You've just become a bore and everybody knows it." She left me standing there with my sweater in my hand.

I was stunned. I couldn't speak. My face grew hot and I felt everybody looking at me. When I looked up I saw Grace and Roy standing at the other side of the auditorium. They were looking in my direction and Grace suddenly started to talk to Roy and neither looked my way again. I don't know how I got through that day at school.

After school I didn't wait for Grace. I hurried out and away from them all. But just as I started up the mountain, Grace overtook me.

"I've thought of something, Shan. I know a way to get ten dollars."

I looked at her without speaking. I was still stunned.

"You know there's a big price at Dave Darby's store for roots and hides and poultry," she said, speaking quickly. "I noticed the sign yesterday. And you know the coves above the gorges are filled with ginseng, yellow root, and May-apple root."

She waited for me to speak. I walked in silence for a while, thinking it was all too late now—thinking I'd sell my sweater for whatever I could get for it.

"When is the note due?" she asked.

"Ten more days," I said. "April twenty-eighth."

"We'll have it by then," she said.

We, I thought. I looked at her and thought of Jo-Anne. Jo-Anne was pretty and gay and popular but her face had changed in my mind. I began to wonder if all that gaiety was real—and what she had meant by "love." I was too puzzled to think anything out.

Grace and I walked along silently. We didn't stop at the gorge because Grace had suggested that we go into the cove. I just followed along and started to hunt ginseng after Grace had started.

I never saw anyone before who could find three-prong and four-prong ginseng like Grace. We found patches of yellow root and Mayapple. We filled our lunch pails with these precious roots and I took them home, strung them the way Mom used to string apples and shuck beans to dry, and hung them on nails driven in the wall above our stove.

We stopped every evening that week and gathered wild roots, and I brought them home to dry. On April twenty-seventh, one day before my note was due—and I had already received the notice—I took a small paper sack of dried Mayapple roots, a small sack of yellow root, and more than a pound of the precious ginseng roots to Dave Darby. When he was through weighing the roots he did some figuring. Then he said, "It all comes to sixteen dollars if you trade it out in the store."

"How much if I take cash?" I asked.

"Fifteen dollars," he said.

"Let me have the cash."

I went straight to the Citizens' State Bank and paid off my note. And I had five dollars for Grace. I never felt better, not even when I was so much in love with Jo-Anne.

As I walked home with Grace I told her how much the roots had brought. "This is not your half," I said as I gave her the five dollars, "but we'll dig more until we get your share. I paid my note."

"Wonderful," she said, smiling at me.

I looked at Grace. Whatever had been wrong with me, I wondered. Why didn't I see before that she had beauty such as Jo-Anne could never have? Grace was as beautiful as our mountain was in April, prettier than a blossom of wild phlox or a mountain daisy. She was as solid as the jutted cliffs, I thought, and as durable as the mountain oaks.

"Now ask me if there is anything more I want from you," I said as I took her arm to help her up the mountain toward the gorge and the wild-root coves.

"What is it?" she asked quickly.

"Take off Roy Tomlinson's sweater," I said. "I'm awfully tired of looking at it."

"But what will I do without it?" she said. "It keeps me warm."

I didn't answer. I started to pull off mine. Then I felt her hand on my arm. "No, Shan," she said. "Keep it a while. I couldn't wear it yet."

We stood silently on the mountain path and looked at each other. "I couldn't wear it yet," she had said. And that was all the promise I needed. I knew how fine she was and I was proud that she would not discard Roy Tomlinson's sweater as Jo-Anne had done, without a word to him first.

I didn't know what she was thinking as we started down the path and she didn't know what I was thinking. I didn't ask her, she didn't ask me. But I was thinking that our high school days would soon be over and I could build a house, if she'd want it there, right on Seaton Ridge on the path that leads from her family's house to mine.

MARTHA
by Ancella R. Bickley

Wiping the sweat from her forehead with a flowered rag, Martha went into her kitchen and got the teakettle of lukewarm water off the stove. Taking the kettle into the bedroom, she set it on the floor by the marble topped dresser, then went back to the kitchen and got the wash basin from the shelf under the sink. She had something special to do and she wanted to be clean and fresh when she started it. Back in the bedroom, she poured the water in the basin and began to take off her blouse. With the blouse halfway over her head, she remembered the picture and let the blouse drop over her shoulders again. She looked at her dead husband's picture on the table by the bed, picked it up, stared at it for a minute, then turned it to the wall. "Don't let no man see you unclothed," her Momma always told her and taught her to turn the pictures of the men relatives to the wall when she bathed.

Martha finished taking her blouse off and dropped her underpants, keeping her petticoat on, its wide straps at the shoulder loose so that she could slip them down when she needed to. White soap bubbles lathered on brown hands, she reached under and around and washed herself, not looking at or touching anything but what she had to. Her bath finished and her clean clothes on, she carried the tea kettle to the stove, then took the basin to the back door and threw the water out watching as it etched a dark spot on the ground.

She put the basin on the shelf under the sink and went back into the bedroom and got her writing tablet and pencil out of the top dresser drawer. Time to write that letter if she was ever going to do it. Back in the kitchen, she moved to the table and sat down. She smoothed its oil cloth cover, then put a piece of newspaper on it and laid her tablet on the paper. That way she would be sure that if there was grease on the table, it wouldn't get on her writing paper. The tablet was just practice paper though. Back in the bedroom lying flat under the big Bible on the top of the dresser was the real writing paper—the paper that she would copy her letter on to mail. Carrie Houston had stopped in town and got the writing paper for her on her way home from work.

Martha sighed and looked around the old-fashioned kitchen with its coal stove and round oak table. When her daughter, May Anna, built the new house next door and moved into it, Martha had stayed on in the old house. She took care of herself by gardening and canning and selling flowers and milk and butter and renting a room to Carrie Houston. I ain't new like that house, Martha thought. This old house and me belong together.

She thought again of the paper that Carrie Houston had gotten for her. It was crisp and straight. A penny a sheet and two cents for an envelope was what it cost.

"Here," Carrie said, when she brought the paper home and handed her a flat paperbag with the paper and envelopes in it. "I brought two sheets of paper and two envelopes so that you'd have an extra in case you mess one up."

She sighed and picked up her pencil. She had decided to

do it so wasn't no point in putting it off any longer.

"Dear Mr. McGhee," she wrote. "I take my pen in hand to send you these few lines. I seen your ad in a colored paper. I'm a widow woman living in her own house. I'm a Baptist and a Republican and I got five grown children that lives close in. I'd be proud to meet you and even might think of getting married if we hit it off. Mail comes to my box on the road if you want to write, or do stop by my place when you can come this way. I live on Anderson Road just off the C & O line at Matthew's Crossing. Just ask for Mrs. Johnson. Anybody along the road can tell you where my house is. Respectfully yours, Martha Johnson."

She stopped and looked over what she had written. Wish May Anna could read this and make sure it's all right she thought. But she knew better than to let on to May Anna what she was doing. May Anna wasn't easy to live around. You had to do things her way or she pitched a fit. This would be sure to make her mad, but Martha squeezed her lips together, grabbed onto her courage and shooed May Anna out of her mind. She read the letter through again. Guess she couldn't do no better. She got up from the table and went into the bedroom to get the good writing paper and envelope. Ought to do it in ink, she remembered, and pulled out the dresser drawer and got one of Pete's old fountain pens. Maybe the bladder is still good, she thought. Back in the kitchen she got the bottle of ink from the top shelf in the kitchen cabinet, stuck the pen point into the ink and carefully pulled out the little lever on the side of the pen, mashing the air out of the bladder. Then she released the lever slowly, allowing the bladder to fill with ink, hope squeezing into her heart the way the ink was squeezing into the pen.

"I guess I'm ready," she whispered to herself, and sitting

down at the table she took out her good paper and slowly began to copy from the tablet.

Carrie took the letter to the post office on the way to work the next day. "You sure you want to do this?" she asked Martha before she left the house, tucking the letter in her pocket after Martha nodded her head yes.

Every day after that Martha went to the mailbox to look for a letter and she had Carrie check for her a second time when she passed the mailbox on her way in from work of an evening. Martha didn't want to take any chances on May Anna's taking the mail out of the box and finding a letter from a strange man to her mother. Martha had never done anything like writing to a stranger before. Why didn't he answer? Maybe he thought it was too forward of her. Maybe ladies didn't do things like that. Maybe it was wrong of her to want something else in these last days of her life, but, Lord, she wanted some response to her letter. Nothing ever came though. After six months, Martha quit looking.

•••

She was out in her garden hoeing beans one summer morning when a stranger came up the road. He was light skinned with a big brown handle-bar moustache curling up on either side of his mouth. He wore a big floppy hat and took it off to fan himself as he stopped in front of her house and called out to her.

"Scuse me, Ma'am. I'm looking for Mrs. Johnson. Can you tell me where she lives?"

"I reckon I'm her. I'm Martha Johnson," she said, pushing her bonnet back and wiping her face with the corner of her gingham apron.

"I'm Jim McGhee. I got your letter and decided to come

on down instead of writing back," he said, gentle brown eyes looking at her with interest.

Flustered, Martha stared at him, heart beating hard under her blouse, consternation and joy warring in her mind. She'd only been hoping for a letter, and here was Jim McGhee instead. She felt almost tongue tied. "You—you —you sure is a man of action," she stammered. "Come on up on the porch and sit a spell. I got some lemonade in the icebox." She leaned her hoe against the side of the house and led the way up on the porch, peeping back over her shoulder to be sure he was following her. She could hardly believe it. He was real and he was here—at her house. The morning glory vines running up on the strings tied to the tacks just under the roof on both sides of the porch gave it an air of coolness and privacy. He walked behind her to the porch and sat in the rocking chair that Carrie Houston usually sat in.

Rocking back and forth and sipping lemonade, he told her how he'd decided to move after his wife died. "We didn't have no children," he said. "Wasn't nothing to keep me up North. I like being married; I'm fifty-five years old, but I just decided that there might be a good Christian woman out there somewhere who might be looking for a man that wasn't afraid of work. Ads sell a lot of stuff and I thought that they might sell me, too. So here I am."

They rocked and talked, exploring each other's lives, tiptoeing around each other's needs. He left to go back to town to look for a job and a place to stay and Martha's head buzzed with excitement. Down inside in the secret places, she was all smiles and warmth. The smiles were still hovering around her heart when Carrie Houston came home from work that night.

"I believe he's a good man, Carrie. Maybe I'll marry him

if he wants me to."

"You sure is a fool, Martha. You just met him. You can't really be thinking about marrying him already—You got him through the mail order!"

"It ain't like I found him in the Sears Roebuck catalog." Martha said tiredly, almost as if she'd said it all before, perhaps to herself. "It was an ad in that colored paper that all the church folks reads. That really don't seem bad, does it Carrie? May Anna and the others got their own life and I'd like to have my own, too, before I die. I know I had Pete and the children, but something inside of me is still empty—been empty all of my life. Even with Pete it was empty. Like I didn't count for nothing. I was always doing and hushing, not being. I don't want to end up my life like this—with me not being. Maybe Jim's the one that can help me find whatever it is I'm looking for."

"What about May Anna? You know she ain't going to want her fancy school teacher friends to know her Momma took up with some man she got through the mail order." Carrie stood, hands on hips shaking her head.

"I guess I won't tell her nothing about what I'm planning until its done. I ain't even goin' to let her know that Jim's here. He'll only come to visit during the day time when she ain't home," Martha replied.

"May Anna gets crazy mad about most anything," she went on. "Sometimes even breaks up dishes and all. They even had to talk to her down at the school about goin' on like that—yellin' at them kids and threatenin' to whip them about the least little thing. You can't never tell what she'll do when she's into one of them fits of her'n. Sometimes, when Pete was still living and she was carrying on, she'd listen to him. I never could do nothing with her, though. Got so, I wouldn't even try. Just let her rare and waited it out."

"I got me a place to stay and a job," Jim told Martha the next time he came to visit. "I'm rooming with Mr. Billy Williams and I'm washing dishes on the evening shift at a restaurant in town. That way, I can keep my days free to visit you."

Jim would come early of a morning, soon as May Anna was gone. Martha wasn't quite sure how to act; she wasn't young and she wasn't good looking. All she had was inside, and scary as it was to let anybody know about that, she decided to try to let him see the her that she'd kept tucked away so long. She would fix him breakfast and they'd sit at the kitchen table sipping coffee out of blue enamel tin cups, talking and talking. Martha always took the cup with the chip. She'd dropped it on the coal stove one day when she was using it to pour water into her pinto beans and had knocked a big piece of the enamel off.

Once, Jim reached across the table and laid his hand over hers, gently touching her knuckles, mis-shapen from arthritis. "Hurt?" he asked quietly.

Martha held her breath for a moment, feeling his hand on hers, her heart pounding like it would jump right out of her chest. "Sometimes," she said. "They ain't very pretty are they?" and she looked ruefully down at her brown hands, swollen, work hardened, skin wrinkled.

"Pretty is as pretty does. I know they done plenty good," Jim replied, his hand stroking hers softly before he picked up his coffee cup once more.

He even offered to wash the dishes for her telling her that he was an expert since that's what he did for a living. Deep inside that surprised and pleased her. A man washing dishes in her kitchen! She liked his asking about the dishes, but she never let him wash them.

"Just you sit and talk to me, and the work'll go fast," she said. "Besides, the warm dishwater makes my hands feel better." She'd pour him another cup of coffee and while she washed the dishes, he'd tell her how his daddy'd sharecropped in Alabama and what it was like living in the city up North. Martha told him things she'd never said to anybody. How she'd cried because she wanted a hair ribbon when she was a little girl and her daddy was too poor to buy it for her, how sad she was when her daddy kept her out of school to help with the chores around the farm, and about that scary dream she always had—where somebody, she never knew who, threw a quilt over her head and held it tight and she was smothering and afraid of the thing over her face and the dark and was crying and screaming and couldn't get them to take it off no matter how she begged. She didn't talk about Pete, and he didn't talk about his wife. It was like they was both starting something new together and they wanted to let the old lay where it was.

Sometimes he'd put his hand on her arm when he came into the kitchen of a morning. "You doing all right today?" he'd ask. "You have that dream last night?" It got so the dream wasn't coming so much and Martha would shake her head, "no," smile and turn to the stove to get their breakfast, ashamed to have him see how glad she was that she'd found him.

On Sundays he'd show up at church—never sat next to her or nothing, just smiled at her and let her know he was there.

"You reckon we know each other well enough to get married?" Jim asked one day after he'd come by about three months.

"I expect so," Martha replied and they went off to Catlettsburg and done it. Wasn't no three day waiting time in

Kentucky like it was in West Virginia. You just went right up to the justice of the peace. They took the bus over.

Martha knew May Anna was gonna act crazy when she found out, but she didn't know how bad it was gonna be. It was a week after they got married that they decided to tell her. Jim had stayed on in his own place in town, but he had asked for a day off and they was sitting on the front porch when May Anna came home from her school teaching job.

"Come over here, May Anna." Martha called when she saw May Anna open the gate and start up the sidewalk toward the big white house. "I got something to tell you."

"Be there soon as I put my books down," May Anna called back and went up the steps to her house and put the books on the porch floor. Turning, she came back down the steps and walked over to the little house. "How're you?" she said to Jim, looking at him suspiciously. Strange men didn't find their way out to Anderson Road very often. "You got any lemonade, Momma?" She sat down on the edge of the porch.

"I'm fine, Ma'am," Jim replied.

"I'll get the lemonade, then we'll talk," Martha said and went inside the house, screen door screeching as she opened it and went through the front room to the kitchen.

"You're not from around here are you? I don't think I've seen you before," May Anna said as she took her handkerchief from her pocket and wiped sweat from her forehead.

"No, Ma'am, I come here from New Jersey."

"Well, you're kind of down South here. You been here long?"

"Little over three months," he replied.

"Here let me help you," he said jumping to his feet to take the pitcher from Martha as she started to back out of the screen door, hands too full with glasses and pitcher to open it.

As Jim put both hands around the aluminum pitcher, pieces of ice clunked into each other and hit against its metal side.

Martha put the glasses on the floor, took the pitcher from Jim, and poured lemonade into them, hands fluttering a bit, uneasily.

"Pass this to May Anna, won't you, Jim?" and she handed him a glass for her daughter, almost sloshing the lemonade over the edge; then she stretched out her hand with a glass for him as he passed the first one on.

"I see you met Jim while I was in the house, May Anna," Martha said as she settled into her rocking chair, her own glass of lemonade gripped tightly in her hand. Better to just say it, she thought. "He's gonna be staying here from now on." Martha could see the look on May Anna's face as she held the glass near her mouth and stared at her over the rim.

"Is he a friend of Miss Carrie's?" May Anna asked.

"No. Me and him got married last week," Martha blurted out.

May Anna choked and spat the lemonade back into the glass. "You what!" she sputtered."

"Got married," Martha said again. "Down in Catlettsburg. We took the bus down and back."

"Married! To this man?" May Anna raised her voice. "Who is he? I never saw him before. You don't even know him! You got more sense than that, Momma."

"Miss May Anna,..." Jim started to explain.

"Who you talking to? Don't you 'Miss May Anna' me. You no account trash."

"He ain't trash, May Anna. He's got him a job and every-thing—lives in town now, but he's gonna go get his things and come back here," Martha tried to go on, anxiety and distress apparent in her voice—wanting to get it all out before May Anna could start talking again.

"He's not staying on this place," May Anna grated, batting her eyes hard and fast like she always did when she was about to go pucker mouth mad.

Turning to Jim she said through her teeth, "Go on, get out of here."

Jim sat looking from one to another.

"Get off this place!"

Martha started to rock, chair going faster and faster, lumpy fingers weaving in and out as she pleated the hem of her apron. May Anna, chest heaving, stood in front of her mother, looking down at her, hands on hips, voice getting louder as she talked.

"You going to give away everything my daddy worked for––to some good for nothing stranger. I won't have it. You tell him to leave or I'll kill him."

When her mother just kept rocking, May Anna picked up the pitcher and threw it at Jim. He jerked his head away. The pitcher just missed his head and clanged against the top of his chair. Lemonade splashed his shoulder and ran down his shirt sleeve and the side of the chair. The ice chunks skittered across the floor of the porch, puddling in the hot sun. He jumped from the chair as May Anna reached for a glass and pulled her arm back to throw.

"May Anna, please stop it!" Martha didn't know what to do. The commotion inside of her matched the commotion on the porch. She put out her hand as if to restrain May Anna. Drew it back. Why'd she ever think she could buck May Anna?

May Anna threw the glass. Jim ducked again. The glass smashed against the wall of the house.

Emotion twisting her face; she looked around for another glass.

"Quit it, May Anna." Martha pleaded.

"Get him out of here," May Anna panted. "I'm going after my gun. If he's here when I come back, I'll shoot him. I swear I will." She turned from the porch and ran toward the big house, disappearing inside.

"You better go, Jim" Martha said. "I'll send you word by Carrie Houston when you can come by."

"You gonna let her do this?" Jim asked. "You mean this is the way it is?"

He looked questioningly at Martha, his heart in his eyes.

"She's crazy when she's like this, Jim. I can't do nothing with her. You better go before she comes back."

May Anna's screen door slammed. She was headed back toward them, shotgun in hand.

Jim looked down at the sleeve of his shirt beginning to dry in the sun, lemonade stains from shoulder to cuff. He picked up his hat, went into the house and out the back door.

•••

On a late summer day, Martha tied her poke bonnet under her chin. She went out her front door, across the porch and down the steps. The stiff brim of her bonnet cupped her face. Wisps of gray hair frizzed across her damp forehead. She went around the corner of the big house, down to the gate where the mail box stood. Dry grass crunched as she walked. No rain for a long time, she thought as she reached for the little trap door that opened the front of the mail box. She stuck her hand in, feeling only tin hottened by the afternoon sun. She stooped a bit, looked in, seeing the bare inside of the arched, cave-like metal container. Then she turned and started slowly back to her house, eyes shaded by the bonnet's starched brim, neck shielded from the sun by the little ruffle gathered at the back.

Inside the house, she looked around at the dim interior. Hot for September, she thought as she stood in the front room and looked bleakly at its window.

Old people, old houses, Martha shrugged as she remembered her last conversation with May Anna. "I want you to get out of that old house." May Anna was pushing hard, especially since Jim. "It's time we tore it down. Miss Carrie can get a room in town. You're getting old. You need to be where there's gas and running water and indoor toilets."

But I got to hang on to my own place, Martha thought. It's been a year, but maybe Jim'll come back or write and tell me where he is and I can go see him and tell him how much I miss him and how sorry I am that I let him go.

After May Anna pitched that fit, it was a while before Jim started coming out again. When he did come back, something had changed between them. They still sat in the kitchen together, eating breakfast and drinking coffee out of the blue enamel cups, and he wanted to help with the dishes like always, but something was different. Martha would turn around sometimes, steam from the dishwater still on her glasses so she couldn't see real good, but it seemed like he'd be watching her with a funny look in his eyes, a sort of sadness. He didn't talk about May Anna. Most days he just sat quiet, not eating much, drinking his coffee, answering her questions. When he got paid, he would leave some money under the sugar bowl. She'd always try to give it back to him next time, but he wouldn't take it. "I'm eating up your food," he said. "I owe you something." It didn't seem like they was ever going to work it out and one day he told her that he had to go to

New Jersey to tend to some business. He was still gone.

How come she couldn't get Jim off her mind? She'd wanted Pete off her mind, but she never told that to anybody. She'd married him to get away from home—from her daddy with too many kids to feed and a hard scrabble farm that kept him poor and made him mean. But it seemed like when she'd married she'd just moved from one bossin' to another—different place, same thing. She'd learned to get along well enough with Pete. He could be all right as long as she kept the place up and done what he told her to as soon as he told it to her. But when he died, she swore she'd never have another man. May Anna was bad enough —telling her what to do all the time.

But then—the yearning took over and she'd found Jim, had him for a little while.

"Why you always let May Anna do you that a way?" Carrie Houston had asked her just last night when they was setting on the porch having their evening pipe after supper. Carrie's rocking chair squeeched comfortingly as she moved back and forth in it.

"I dunno." Martha told her. "May Anna's the baby. We didn't think she was going to live when she was born. To keep her from crying and fussing, I just got used to doing whatever she wanted. She just grew up having her way all of the time and raising sand if she was crossed."

"That didn't give her no leave to run Jim off. She might not a liked him, but she didn't have to run him off."

Shaking her head sadly, Martha walked through the front room. Picking up a paper fan off the table by the front door, she went out on the porch and sat down in the slatted rocking chair. She looked at the brown faces of the mother and child on the fan, "Compliments of Washington's Funeral

Home." Funerals. Wonder if Jim's dead. Maybe God was punishing her for being selfish and wanting something old ladies wasn't supposed to have. Maybe May Anna was God's agent.

"Miss May Anna's holding all the cards," Jim said when Martha finally got around to bringing it up with him just before he stopped coming by. "This is your place and hers. I ain't got nothing to give you but me and the work I can do, but I don't aim to take nothing that's your'n. You got to decide what you want to do."

Once he asked if she would move to New Jersey with him. She said she reckoned not. Much as she wanted to, she couldn't leave her home and go to a strange place.

Martha went over and over everything that had gone on between her and Jim and tried to figure out why she'd done what she did. Why she couldn't hold on to what seemed to be right at her fingertips. She wondered if May Anna really would have shot Jim. Maybe I should have told May Anna she'd have to shoot me if she shot him. Maybe standing up to May Anna about staying on in my own house took all of the starch out of me. Maybe May Anna made me doubt Jim. Maybe I didn't fight her because I got him through the mail order and I was ashamed of it. Maybe I already had all I deserved out of life.

Oh, God! she thought. It was so hard to bear. All Jim would a done was be company for her. But when she was honest with herself, she knew that she wanted more than company. She didn't hardly know how to think about that part of it. How could she think it, how could she say it. She wanted touching and talking and soul and body togetherness. She remembered how Jim'd laid his hand on her arm, how he'd touched her hand. She'd seen the last of fifty. Maybe it was all right for a girl to be this way, but she had grandchildren—why now? She ached for Jim.

It wasn't seemly for a grown woman to feel this a way. She spread her hands and looked at her knuckles all bunched out and hurtin' stiff from arthritis. Jim had helped her see beyond—past the ugliness and the pain. She turned her hands every which way, looking at the fingers and remembering his hands on hers as she held the blue cup. Hands was for working, but they was good, too, for holding and touching. When your kids was all grownup and you didn't have nobody else, what living thing did you get to touch?

Sometimes her son brought little Ola Mae and the others by to see her and she got to touch them. Baby people and baby chicks. Sometimes when she had baby chicks, she'd go get the least chick, the runt of the lot, and hold it in her hand and stroke it with a finger, relishing the warmth and life of it. She'd carry it around in her apron pocket and take it out when she sat on the porch in her rocker. She never even told Carrie Houston that. But she did tell Jim.

She waved at her face with the funeral home fan and dozed, and pumped the rocker. Late day sun came through the morning glory vines, warm like Jim's hand on her arm.

"Evening, Martha." Carrie Houston stepped up on the porch, took off her big straw hat and plopped down in the other rocking chair.

"Howdy, Carrie. You had a hard day?"

"No. Miz Silverton was gone most of the day, and I just did up the ironing. Worst part was walking here from the bus stop. You had a good day?"

"I bcen thinking a lot about Jim," Martha told her. "Went down to the mailbox in all that sun to see if I got a letter from him."

"He write?"

"No. Wasn't nothing in the mailbox. Just a handful of hot."

"You got to quit thinking about it. Looks like you and him can't never live together here. You ready to go off with him if he come back?"

"You know I can't leave this place. It's all I got—onliest way I can have any living at all is to stay here. Jim ain't really got no place for us to go—just a room here, nothing up North. Ain't no other place I want to live anyway. All my kids was born here. It's my home. It could be me and Jim's home.

They rocked in silence for a moment.

"Beats me, Martha, how you take on so about Jim McGhee. You past fifty years old. You near 'bout an old lady. We all got to make peace with that.

"Still lonesome on the inside, I guess."

The katydids began their evening song, background music to the squeaking of the rocking chairs.

"I don't know what come over me. The first time Jim come here, I was out in the garden with the hoe. Not cleaned up nor nothing. We took to each other right away. Law, how we talked. I never done that with Pete. Then we run off like kids—down to Catlettsburg and got married," she mused as if trying to explain her actions to herself.

"I know. I know." Carrie soothed. "You sorry about it?"

"I dunno. I still ain't figured it out. Maybe I'll know someday before I die. I guess nothing else was ever intended in my life. Maybe this is all there is. All there was supposed to be, and I couldn't change it. I wanted to, and for a little bit, I thought I could. But when it come right down to putting myself and my wants up front, much as I wanted to, I just couldn't do it. I couldn't. I guess Jim knowed that 'fore I did, and that's why he didn't come back or write." She rocked in silence.

"You et already? " she asked.

"No. Since I was out to the place by myself most of the day and didn't cook no dinner for the family, wasn't much to eat."

"There's greens on the stove. Beets on the table. Pork chops and cornbread in the oven. Get you some. Come back and sit. It's too hot inside."

"I don't mean to be eating up your food…."

"There's plenty left."

Carrie sat for a minute longer, rocker moving slowly. "I'll have some then. Be back directly." She disappeared into the house.

Martha pulled her pipe out of her apron pocket, lit it and swayed back and forth in the rocker. Before her, the big house loomed in the evening sun. May Anna, standing near one of the upstairs windows, looked out at her mother sitting on the porch and then lowered the shade.

MISSING IN ACTION IN APPALACHIA
by James M. Gifford

We were putting up hay. By noon, it was close to 95°, and we had all taken off our shirts and left them in the cab of the truck. My ten-year-old brother Tommy proudly drove the truck slowly through the field, so that my Dad, James Stone, and his brother Robert and I could throw the seventy-pound hay bales on the old weathered farm wagon hitched behind the aging truck.

As many times as I had seen him stripped to the waist, I still couldn't keep from staring at the angry red welts that covered Uncle Robert's back and chest.

According to Dad, "Robert had been a real hell raiser when he was a boy" and had been in five knife fights and one gun battle—mostly over women.

Robert noticed our stares and with a wink he turned to Tommy and said "Boys, there's big money to be made on knife scars!"

"How, Uncle Robert?" Tommy asked in his little boy voice.

"Well boys, I'm going to a tatoo parlor down in Pikeville this weekend. I'm going to have Pikeville tatooed here," he said, indicating the end of a long scar on his chest, "and I'll put Paintsville here and over here on my shoulder it'll say Ashland. Why boys, I can go to work for the state government as a road map of Eastern Kentucky!"

Tommy and I laughed and Dad rolled his eyes. Uncle Robert didn't say much about his fights only because Dad and Mom had both told him it would be a bad influence on "two impressionable boys."

So the conversation turned to sports.

"Young John's a hoss," I heard Uncle Robert say.

"Well, maybe a little hoss," Dad replied.

I did not turn to look at my Dad or my Uncle Robert. I knew Dad's face was stoic, but that his eyes and slight smile betrayed his great pride in me.

I was only sixteen years old, but I was 6' 4" and weighed 217 lbs. I had been starting forward on my high school team since I was a freshman. Now in the summer after my junior year, I was beginning to get letters and telephone calls from college coaches. Every day was exciting, but Dad kept me from getting "the big head."

My Dad was still a local legend. He had played college ball for a year before he left school and married my Mom. Although he was forty years old, he could still beat me in a game of "horse." But he could no longer beat me one-on-one. He was "only" 6' 2" and 200 lbs, so I could "back him into the paint" and score over him—most of the time.

He had taught me how to rebound when I was first falling in love with the game.

"Use your butt, Johnny! Push your man out of position," he said with the quiet confidence of a man who knew exactly what he was talking about. "You get rebounds on the floor, not in the air," he continued.

I knew what he meant. As I got bigger and older, I learned

to play a physical game. I loved to bang into Dad and anybody else who wanted to challenge me. Farm work had made me tough.

My priorities changed during the summer of 1966. I didn't mind the work—and I loved to outwork "grown men"—but I just couldn't concentrate on milk cows and hay bales.

When I was working—or for that matter when I was in school or in church—all I thought about was basketball and Sue Stanley.

Sue hated her name. She said she'd rather be a "Marilyn" or a "Debbie" or even a "Sandra."

"Sue is such an ordinary name," she often confessed to me in private.

We told each other everything. We had known each other since the first grade. We rode the school bus together. We were in many of the same classes in high school. Our families attended the same church. We were so close. After we got old enough to realize what love was, we realized that we had been in love for a long time.

Our senior year was a blur. We graduated in June of 1967, and I was filled with uncertainty. Would I marry Sue right away, or would we wait until after college? Would I go to a big school and play shooting forward or a smaller school, where I could play power forward?

All of that uncertainty ended when my uncle offered me a job. My uncle—Uncle Sam—had a job for me in Vietnam, and my heart leaped at the chance to follow in the footsteps of the men in the Stone family—men who had all served in the military as far back as the American War for Independence.

According to Dad's mother, Granny Stone, "Stone men fought for American freedom from the git go."

A shade-tree genealogist, Granny Stone "allowed as how Stones had fought at Cowpens, marched with Andy Jackson, fought the Indians and Mexicans just to get ready for the Civil War."

"Lord, Lord, don't get me started on the Civil War," she continued with all the enthusiasm of our preacher at altar call. "We had boys on both sides."

At other times, she regaled me with stories of relatives "who marched with Teddy" and fought in WWI and WWII. "Why your second cousin Billy got a toe froze off in Korea," she once observed with what seemed to be a fair amount of pride.

•••

I spent eight weeks of basic training at Fort Campbell. Then I took AIT, Advanced Individual Training, at Fort Leonard Wood. Right before my unit left for Vietnam, I caught pneumonia. When I got out of the hospital, I was assigned to a placement unit. While I was waiting for orders, I did funeral details. That upset me so much that I put in my 1049 transfer request and eventually received orders to go to Vietnam.

Four weeks later, I was locked up at Travis Air Force Base in Oakland. The AWOL rate there was so high that we didn't get to go out and see San Francisco. At 3 a.m., a Second Lieutenant, who looked much younger than me, woke us up. "Make your calls, boys. You're going to war," he said with a maturity that did not match his youthful appearance.

We flew from Travis to Anchorage, Alaska, and then on to Tokyo, where we changed pilots. From there we flew to Tonsenook in South Vietnam, where I spent two days on a "detail unit." Then I boarded a C130 for Chuly where I served for a year with the First Aviation Brigade. I was surrounded by death. The horror filled my mind, and I spent most of my energy trying to stay alive—and stay sane.

I wrote to Sue every week and she wrote to me at least twice a week. I don't think I would have survived Vietnam without her.

When I got back to the states, I was a different person. I felt hollow. I felt lost on the farm. I loved my family and I still loved Sue. Every morning, I woke hoping that this would be the day I became the happy, optimistic person I once was.

After a year of feeling lost and out of place, I packed a suitcase one Sunday morning. Mom and Dad were at church, so I left them a note, and I left a note for them to give to Sue. I began hitchhiking west toward I-75.

I just didn't know what to do with my life. I felt so conflicted. I wanted to step back into my "real life," the life I had before Vietnam. But I couldn't. I simply could not be that person again.

So I wandered the South for ten years, supporting myself well with construction work. And every day I wanted to go back home and marry Sue. I called her every week for the first six years I was gone. Even after she married, I still loved her. At night, I couldn't stop myself from thinking about her. I desperately wanted to pick her up at home and hold her hand on the way to the movies and kiss her goodnight in the dark shadows of her front porch. Sometimes I felt like I would die from the emptiness of being away from her.

One spring day in 1980 I called her from a pay phone in Murfreesboro, Tennessee. "I'm coming home, sweetheart. I'm going to ride the Greyhound Bus into Knoxville tonight and take a bus to Lexington tomorrow. My bus arrives at 3 p.m. Can you pick me up? Will that cause problems for you at home?"

"Johnny," she said in a voice that always seemed to be the sound of love, "I got bad news. Your mom is real sick.... I'll pick you up tomorrow."

Mom was dying when I walked up the steps to the house where I was raised. Dad and I sat with her while she passed into the eternal life that I knew was her reward for a life of incredible goodness and sacrifice.

A week later, I drove Dad's truck to town and had a few beers with some "boys" I had played ball with in high school. At eleven o'clock that night, I was saying my goodbyes when three mean-spirited drunks stormed into the dimly lit room that my Mom had always called that "horrible honky tonk."

One of them pointed a gun at the bartender and demanded all the money in the till.

The other two stood facing the four remaining patrons. They screamed and cursed and waved their guns like crazy men.

"Boys," I said, "don't ruin your lives. I've got $110 in my pocket that I'll loan you! Then you won't have to rob this place!"

I looked at the guy who seemed to be in charge and he nodded his head slightly.

I went to my back pocket for my wallet, and then I felt the impact that I had feared for thirteen months in Vietnam. I felt a burning sensation and I guess I slumped in my chair.

Blood soaked my jeans and ran down into my boots. I wasn't thinking very well. I wasn't sure whether I was in Vietnam or at home.

The room began to spin and I could not see anyone's face very clearly. Then I saw Sue Stanley's face shining through all my pain.

"Sue, I love you," I said. But I couldn't hear myself speak.

•••

The days that followed were a nightmare of sadness for the extended Stone family. James' wife Martha had just died and now he had to bury his son John.

That terrible night when James and his son Tommie had gone to town with Sheriff Bomar to identify the body, the Sheriff gave James his son's personal effects.

It wasn't until after the funeral that James sat down at the kitchen table where he and Martha had shared breakfast for thirty-one years and carefully examined the contents of the small manila envelope that was all that he had left of his eldest son.

He had to stop and remind himself that he wasn't violating his son's privacy when he went through his wallet. He took $110 from the wallet and decided that he would give the money to Tommie.

Then he opened a warn, tattered, blood-stained envelope and found a letter that haunted him for the rest of his life. He read it over and over again, crying till there were no more tears left in him.

July 18, 1975
Knoxville, Tennessee

Dear Sue,

I'm in East Tennessee, not all that far from home. I'm working for a construction company that's building college dormitories, and we've got to finish before the kids get here for the fall semester. So we're working ten hours a day, seven days a week.

I'm working with a good crew, and I'll tell you about them when I get home.

I don't know why it has taken me so long to get my mind right, but I know I want to come home this fall and marry you. I know you've heard that before, but I mean it.

I love you with all my heart. I'll build a home for us on the ridge behind Dad's barn. You know the place!

You won't have to work anymore—unless you just want to. I want to make your life easier. I want you to enjoy making a home for us.

Let's build a house with plenty of room for you to plant flowers and have a nice lawn, because I know that pleases you.

Sue, I know I've caused you so much grief, but if you will make a 100% commitment to marriage, I will do the same. If you will devote your energy and love to me, then I will do the same. Let's spend the rest of our lives being happy and healthy together.

Sue, you're the only girl I've ever loved. Let's build on the best days of our past and make a life together.

I've been thinking about this for a long time, so I know how I feel. I hope you still feel the same way.

I realize that I have one advantage to this proposal. I know how much you like to decorate! Now you'll have a home of your own to paint and paper.

Seriously, I love you. Please marry me.

Love,
John

Every day for the rest of his life—and he lived another nineteen years after the terrible year when Martha and John died—James Stone wondered what his son's life would have been if he had mailed that letter.

And every day for the rest of her life, Sue wondered what her life would have been if Johnny Stone, the love of her life, had mailed that letter.

She never told her husband or her children about the letter which Johnny's Dad gave to her after Church—he waited till she was alone—a month after Johnny's funeral. She knew it would make Garland sad, and her boys just wouldn't understand.

So she kept the letter in a locked box in her desk. Each morning, after Garland and the boys left, she fixed herself a cup of coffee and sat down at her desk to read the letter and think about her life.

"Everyone has secrets," she would say to herself as she returned the letter to its private resting place.

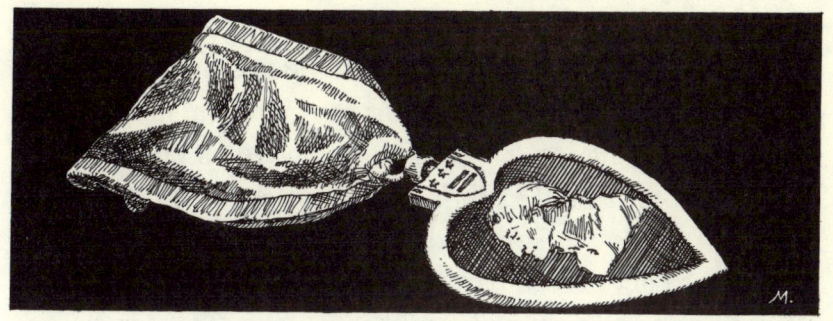

BEN PAXTON'S HEART
by Jimmy Lowe

He was late, very late, and he was in a hurry. The elevator was being cleaned, so he had to take the stairs. He tried to leap up two steps at a time like he did when he was a high school quarterback. But that was thirty-three years ago, and now his belt was tight and his breathing labored.

"Sir? Sir? Do you need help?"

Who was talking? He tried to focus: a teenage girl with dark hair and green eyes—what was she doing above him?

"You stay right here. Don't try to get up. I'll go call 911."

Why 911? Is there an emergency? He tried to ask her, but she was gone, and he found he couldn't make himself talk, anyway.

He was hurting. What happened? He tried to think.

"Sir, an ambulance is on the way." The girl was back, her face above his. She looked worried, and this made him concerned for her. He wanted to reassure her that everything was okay, and he reached out to take her hand, but there was fire in his chest and arm. Her face, with those beautiful green eyes, faded from him like bad television reception. She was saying something else, but she was far, far away.

Those eyes. Now he remembered. Shelia?

After the sun went down there was a cool breeze that passed through the car. With both windows down the night air felt sweet to the skin that had been burned in the hayfield most of the day. Ben's back felt awkward as he sat in the front seat of his 1961 Ford Fairlane. He squirmed a bit from time to time to get some relief. Once he twisted in such a way that he actually made his back pop. Shelia giggled at the sound and he felt embarrassed; still, it gave some temporary relief to his back.

"Do you want something from the concession stand? Popcorn? Coke? Anything?"

"No, not really. You go get some, if you want, though," Shelia said.

He didn't go. He didn't really want anything, either; he just wanted an excuse to go to the restroom and take off his shirt. He wanted to rub his back where it was itching so. His sunburn would soon start peeling.

The little white speaker that hung on the left side of the car door announced, "Show starts in five minutes!" Then there were the usual cartoon figures dancing to "Let's all go to the lobby...Let's all go to the lobby."

Ben scooted in the front seat over to Shelia's side. He was so close now he could hear her breathing. He needed to say something important tonight. It was time. He had been thinking about it all day as he had lifted the bales and put them on the wagon for his brother to place while their father drove the tractor. He had been thinking about it so much that his dad had gotten on him about not having his mind on his work. His brother only laughed, having a pretty good idea of what Ben was up to.

For a week or more Ben had been as indecisive as Hamlet. He had even tried the Benjamin Franklin idea: dividing a

sheet of paper in half, on the left side he listed all the cons
and on the right, all the pros. Finally he had come to a conclusion—the conclusion that his life had naturally been leading toward: he would marry Shelia and settle down next to
his parents. After all, she was a pretty girl, with the most
beautiful green eyes he had ever seen.

Why had that decision been so difficult?

"It's sure been hot today," he said. Now, that was stupid.
Why do people always comment on the weather as if it were
supremely interesting? Sure, it was hot today. Shelia lived in
Kentucky, just three miles down the road from him. She knew
what July was like. She had been outside today. How utterly
stupid. Yet, it had been said. It was out there now. And now
she would feel compelled to respond in some way. Why hadn't
he just said, "This is the sound of my voice. I hope you find it
warm and appealing, because I really want to connect with
you. Let me hear your voice."?

Sure enough, she said something.

"Yes."

"What?"

"Yes, it was hot today."

"Well, it's cooled off now." Gosh! He did it again. How
dumb! Where can a conversation like this possibly go?

"Yes," she said.

At least he held off this time from making any more ob-
vious weather observations.

A moth flew into the car. He took the showbill and waved
it on through. Then the movie started. Lit up on the screen
were Henry Fonda and Maureen O'Hara and the big family of
young'uns in "Spencer's Mountain." They watched in silence.

He had wanted to go away to college like the boy in
the movie. Mrs. Cooke had tried to get him to fill out a

financial aid application. She had told him about grants that were available. She had told him he had a fine mind, and that was really something, coming from the toughest English teacher in the school.

"Ben, we need you on the farm," his father had said when he mentioned college. "You'll farm the land, like I have, and my own father did, and his father before him and so on. Right now you've got more education than any of the rest of us. It's time you put the schoolbooks away and became a man. Marry Shelia. We'll build you a little place on the hollow. In time, maybe you can buy some acreage off Old Man Thompson. He doesn't have any children and he's getting on up in years."

Surely his dad had been right. Farming was hard work, but he could do it. Shelia was a fine girl. He had known her all his life. Anyway, it was all right there on paper: the list on the right side was the longest. Still….

He looked over at Shelia, her face in the glow of the drive-in Technicolor. She would make a good wife. His dad was right. It was just that he had yearned to go places that looked different than the hills around home, read all the books in the library—and wouldn't it be something to be a teacher like Mrs. Cooke?

He decided to get on with it. "Sheila, I've been thinking…."

She turned her face from the screen toward him. "What have you been thinking, Ben?"

"Well, we're both out of school now, and maybe it's time to, ah, well, what I've been thinking is, since we've…."

"Are you proposing to me, Ben?" she teased.

"Well, I guess I am. Yes, I am." She made it so easy for him. In a gush he said, "Let's get married."

"Yes," she said, and Ben looked at the screen. What now? Henry Fonda was getting fresh with Maureen O'Hara. He looked back to Shelia. It seemed he should at least kiss her. He leaned in her direction where she was willing.

"Let's live somewhere far away from these hills. Let's fly in airplanes and see the country of Shakespeare and Thomas Hardy."

"Don't be crazy, Ben. Where would we get that kind of money? Besides, everything we need is right here."

"Wouldn't you like to see what's out there beyond the hills? Someday people may go to the moon—surely we could get across the ocean."

"Those books have filled your head with too many fancy notions, Ben. We'll find a place somewhere between our parents and raise our own family."

He wanted to talk to her of dreams and of passions and of all the great ideas books had opened for him. He wanted to scream, "I want more!", but instead, he heard himself submitting, "I guess you're right, Shelia."

She smiled and looked at him with those green eyes. She was a good-looking girl, he reminded himself, and she had said, "yes."

"Sir? Sir? They're here. Can you hear me?"

"What?"

The girl wasn't Shelia. Who was she? Who was here?

Now other figures loomed above him. They both wore light blue and had on those skin-tight gloves like the janitors did when they cleaned the school restrooms.

Someone undid his belt and opened his shirt. Someone else slipped something cold onto his chest. The awful hurting was back—or had it ever gone away? What was happening? He closed his eyes.

He was floating in the air on a magic carpet—no, it was a surfboard. Where were the waves? Then he landed in a small room. Someone told him, "We're going to take care of you. Just hold on, now." The little room began to move. There was a siren from somewhere. Maybe someone had been caught speeding.

There had been sirens when he had returned home from Vietnam. He had received the purple heart for a wound he took during action. It healed okay, but left him with a limp and he was sent home early. The community gave him a hero's welcome, complete with police escort. And then he met Julie.

"Call me Ben," he had told her after she had started to address him with "Mister" and then stumbled into "Sergeant."

"You are my first interview for *The Times*. I just got the job last Monday."

She had asked him about the war and his wound and his homecoming. He answered each question politely, but his thoughts weren't completely on the interview. When he could, he asked her a few questions, and he learned she had just graduated from the state college with a journalism degree.

Julie was a little short and Ben wondered where she would strike him if they stood together. His shoulder? He was attracted to this girl and this made him feel guilty. It was Shelia he should be thinking of. They had put their marriage plans off by mutual consent due to the draft. But now it was time to get on with it.

"I hope I haven't taken too much of your time," Julie said after an hour's worth of the interview. "It's just that I was hoping to do an in depth piece, one that maybe the AP wire would pick up. And I do find you quite interesting, Mr.—ah, Ben." Was she blushing? Ben thought she was but he didn't want to stare. Then he couldn't help himself. She was lovely. He met her eyes. She seemed so passionate about getting the story. From somewhere as far away as Asia he heard himself say, "How about having dinner with me tomorrow night?" Her face immediatley broke open a smile. He quickly added, "You know, for the opportunity to continue the interview." She said, "Oh." Did he detect some disappointment? Anyway, she had accepted, and the following evening he and Julie had their first meal together.

He hadn't laughed for the past eight months. Now he was making up for all those tense times. Julie listened as he told about an incident on the plane home about a clumsy steward who had accidentally spilled beer in his lap. The steward had profusely apologized and presented him with a voucher for a free round-trip ticket to anywhere in the world served by that airline within the next year.

"Where do you think you will go?" Julie asked with great curiosity.

"Somewhere other than Vietnam—that's for sure."

"I know where I'd go," she said.

"Where?"

"Paris."

"Have you ever been there?"

"Not yet, but I'll go someday. I want to go almost everywhere someday. I think travel and real-life experiences are the greatest education one can achieve."

She scooted closer to him from across the table as she talked of her hopes to meet people from all over the world. Someday she hoped to write a novel, but first she wanted to taste as much of the world as possible. Ben was enchanted.

He felt something light on each of his shoe tops. Julie's feet didn't quite reach the floor and she was scotching herself with his feet. He smiled at this realization and he smiled at the pleasant conversation that Julie offered.

The situation with Shelia would have to be re-evaluated.

When their meal had ended and when Julie obviously had enough material for a two-part feature story, their excuse for being together was over. Each thanked the other for a nice evening, and then Julie simply said, "I like you, Ben."

The admission had taken Ben a bit by surprise, but the biggest surprise was his response, "I like you more."

"Mr. Paxton, do you remember me? Maxine Palmore—Maxine Cooper when you had me in lit class."

He studied her face. Yes, she did look familiar.

"You were the best teacher I ever had, Mr. Paxton. When they brought you in, I told them, 'We've got to take special care of this man'."

Ben now realized he was in a hospital. His arm itched, and when he looked across to it, he noticed the IV. He was sore.

"You gave us quite a scare, Mr. Paxton," Nurse Maxine was saying, "but the doctors are satisfied that you are going to be okay. The surgery went just fine."

"Where's my wife?" Ben asked.

"She's been here all the time, Mr. Paxton. She just stepped out a few minutes ago to get a sandwich downstairs. She'll be back any time." Someone else came into the room. He carried a chart and made a few notes. Ben heard the nurse tell the man with the chart something about the Pulitzer Prize Mrs. Paxton had won a few years ago. They talked on for awhile about hospital business, but Ben ceased to hear them. Now his attention was focused on the light footsteps that were walking his way. Then he saw her.

"I love you," she said.

"I love you more."

BUTTONS AND BOWS
by James B. Goode

She came skipping down the steep, graveled road. Her thin yellow and white checked gingham dress swung back and forth as she raised one leg and then the other in short, staccato steps. She whistled "Buttons and Bows" over and over. The late evening summer air was sweet with the smell of red and orange honeysuckle growing on the chicken wire fence along Crittie Grogan's back lot.

He was busy with a crew of men who were setting out hedge along the front row of houses in Machine Shop Hollow in the Black Mountain coal camp. He turned, rested his long arms on the dirt shovel, and watched her slide in the loose gravel as she continued down the hill and disappeared around the curve at the end of the mine car shop. Even after she was gone, little puffs of dust hung just above the road bed and curled around like wisps of smoke from a dying fire.

"Lance!" Someone called from the hedge row. He turned his head toward the sound. Ray, his youngest crew member, winked at Skinny Taylor, who was hefting a carefully pruned hedge into the hole they had just finished.

"Why's an old man like you lookin' at a young girl like that?" Ray said as he pushed his cap back, scratched just above his left ear, and screwed his mouth down on both corners as if to say, "It's way beyond me...."

"I wasn't lookin' at nothin'!" He said.

"Besides that, I ain't but twenty-five-year-old." He blushed, stuck the shovel into a dirt pile and flipped a sand rock aside.

•••

He had known her for over five years. In the spring and summer, Alta and several boys and girls from the hollow came to watch the crew set out trees, plant flowers, build rock walls, construct fences, and dig drainage ditches. Lance worked with his crew all over the camp, but he was more often in the Machine Shop Hollow section because it had the most houses. Their job was to keep the camp landscaped and beautified. He held a contract with the coal company who paid him a lump sum and he, in turn, hired and paid all his men. At first he didn't pay much attention to her. She was just one of the kids. Sometimes the guys would give them a piece of cake or a moon pie from their lunch buckets as they took their breaks and sat with their backs against the shade trees along the hollow road.

He liked to kid her because she was easily flustered.

"Come over here and stand sideways, stick your tongue out and you'll look like a zipper!" He'd say.

"I guess when you were a baby, they had to hang a porkchop around your neck to get the dog to play with you!" He would declare.

"Tell them ugly sisters of yours that I've got a half-dozen ears of corn that they could eat through my picket fence, if they want to!" Lance would do a "chipmunk" thing with his teeth when he got to the "picket fence" part. This made Alta madder than a wet hen. She would begin to cry and flail at him with her fists. He would just hold her thin arms and let out a deep belly laugh. She would storm off, stomping her feet into the dusty road as she marched toward home to tell Ida Mae, her momma, the terrible, awful things he had said to her.

He knew her daddy too. Rome Parsons was the foreman in the company machine shop and was known as the best machinist in eastern Kentucky. Given the right tools, he could repair or make most anything he wanted in that shop. But he had a reputation for liking moonshine whiskey, and camp rumors had it that he was just plain mean when he drank.

Ida Mae was the prettiest woman in the Black Mountain coal camp. People said she was half Cherokee and half French-Canadian. She had long, straight black hair, dark skin, and a slender, muscular build. She was known as a gentle, kind, Christian woman.

Rome and Ida Mae had three girls--Pauline, Rose, and Alta. Alta was the oldest. She wasn't the prettiest. She was too skinny and had inherited high cheek bones and a slightly hooked nose from somewhere deep in her Indian genes. Her legs and arms were long and delicate but out of proportion with the rest of her body.

•••

One early Fall day, shortly after her sixteenth birthday, Alta sat down beside Lance under a Catalpa tree just behind her house and they shared a piece of chocolate cake. Lance had sent the crew to the supply house to get a load of sand and cement just so he could get a chance to talk to her without their prying eyes and ears. The soft light from the sun reflecting in a pool of water in the road made her hair glow and her gray eyes shine like bright silver. He noticed that her figure was beginning to round out and she had begun to use a little rouge on those high cheek bones, which made her look like one of the models he'd seen in the Sears and Roebuck catalog.

"I know your sister Vada!" She blurted out to break an awkward silence. "She's got pretty red hair and blue eyes! She's in my class at school and she's real smart."

"Yes, she has my mother's hair and eyes," Lance said. "Mother came from Loch Ern in Scotland. All her people have red hair and blue eyes." He stretched out his legs, rolled onto his left hip, and faced her. He could see his heart moving the front of his shirt. He had been trying to get the courage to ask her to go with him to the coal company clubhouse and get an ice cream cone but he was afraid. He was nine years older than Alta. Everyone would gossip. After all, he was the most eligible bachelor in Black Mountain and several women his age wanted to date him.

He had put off getting married and having his own family. His father had died just as he was finishing high school and left him to support his Mother and eight brothers and sisters. This was at the beginning of World War II and he had gotten an exemption for being the eldest sole supporting son. He had finally gotten all the boys in the Navy and the girls married off. Now, he was ready to get on with his life.

"Alta, how'd you like to go with me to church Saturday and then have ice cream at the company club after?" Sweat broke out on his upper lip. His tongue and mouth were dry. What if he got turned down by a sixteen-year-old girl? Wouldn't that make the crew laugh and make fun of him? He could just hear Ray and Skinny.

"Tried to rob the cradle, did you? Little baby turn you

down?" They would ride him hard and put him up wet. But he was going to take his chances. He had been living his life for everyone else—now he was going to live some for himself.

She looked at him for a long time. Finally, she leaned over and wiped the dust from the toes of her shoes and carefully cleared her throat.

"I ain't never dated yet and I don't know if Momma will let me go. I'll have to ask her. She might, since we'd be goin' to church. She's real religious and likes for us to go to Sunday school and church." She stood up and smoothed her dress. She reached out with her thumb and tenderly straightened a lock of his black hair, which had fallen down low on his forehead.

"The one I got to worry about the most is Daddy." She said. "Sometimes I think he hates boys worse than he hates city folks."

Lance rolled over on his back and stared at the clumps of long beans on the catalpa. A slight breeze had kicked up, coming up the hollow in gentle waves. The fan-like leaves turned over and fluttered.

"I'll be back up to finish this job tomorrow. Could you meet me down here for dinner and let me know what they say? I'll pack extra sandwiches and cake, if you'll bring a quart of cold buttermilk from Ida Mae's spring house."

Lance watched Alta's cute figure as she went back up the hill toward the little yellow bungalow which sat just below the road leading up to the mine opening. He was hopeful. But he knew that almost every weekend Rome hit the bottle and didn't quit until late Sunday evening. When he drank, he was difficult to get along with. Lance had heard rumors that Rome was mean to Ida and the girls.

He knew that he would give Alta a hard row to hoe.

•••

The next day was Friday and just after noon Alta appeared on the porch of the bungalow and slowly walked toward the rock wall they were building at the Massey house just down the hollow road. The crew started whispering and snickering. Skinny poked and shoved at Lance's shoulder.

"There she is, Lance, another youngun' to raise!" Ray twisted his face in a contortion of exaggerated winking.

As Alta came closer, Lance noticed she was crying. He could see that her face was streaked and tiny wisps of her hair stuck to her flushed cheeks. He dropped his trowel, walked toward her, took her by the hand, and led her over behind one of the mine buildings where they could talk.

"Daddy's drunk as a hoot owl and he said that I wasn't goin' nowhere, especially not with a boy and Ida Mae said I was only goin' to church with one of the most honorable men in the camp and he told her you were worthless and he wasn't goin' to put up with no grown man tryin' to steal his baby and then he yelled at Momma and then he hit her! Told her you were a vulture, always circlin' his house waitin' for his girls to come out of the house." She was sobbing. Her shoulders shook like the catalpa leaves in the mountain breeze.

Lance could feel the anger rise in his chest. His neck and ears got hot and he clenched his teeth. He felt so torn by his anger for Rome and his love for Alta. She had told him of the many times Rome had come home drunk and gotten her sisters and her from their warm beds at two o'clock in the morning and made them sing songs for his drunk buddies who gathered in the kitchen to have a final drink before staggering home to their fretful wives. Lance picked her up, placed her on his strong lap and cradled her.

"Hush, now." He gently whispered over and over until she was quiet.

"We're goin' to church Saturday and then, I don't care what anybody thinks, we're going to walk right down the hill, into the club house, sit down on one of those red leather stools, and order the biggest vanilla ice cream cone you've ever eaten!" Lance hugged her tighter and tighter.

Alta snuggled into his shoulder and sighed. She could smell the faint odor of cigar tobacco and shaving lotion. She caught a whiff of the peppermint candy he kept to give the kids from the hollow. He was a good, gentle man. She began to think about the sight of them strolling to the clubhouse without a care in the world—right in front of everyone. She could picture a vanilla ice cream cone two feet tall and she began to giggle and pretty soon they both were laughing.

"If Ida Mae don't mind, little lady, you go ahead and get your dress clothes on early and I'll be parked down here behind this building about six-thirty." She looked at his handsome face. His face was tan and weathered from working outdoors and a short, black shadow of beard glistened in the noonday sun.

"Daddy will probably still be gone...." She said as she twisted a lock of her hair between her thumb and index finger. "He and Harvey are usually at Bovich's Tavern in Poor Fork until dark thirty!"

•••

As Alta ran up the hill, she felt as light as the hen feathers that floated down from the rafters in the chicken house when she gathered the eggs. Ida Mae was in the kitchen when she burst through the screen door at the back of the house, letting it slam hard behind her.

"Lord, Alta! How many times have I told you not to let that door close so hard." Ida Mae said from her place in front of the double bowl sink where she was cleaning a chicken for supper.

"Momma! Oh, Momma!" She danced around on the flowered linoleum. "He still wants me to go with him to church tomorrow!" She exclaimed.

Ida Mae turned to watch Alta's feet dance across the floor.

"You know you already got us in trouble with Daddy. He yelled and nearly shook the stuffin' out of me the other day because of Lance Tolliver!" she said.

Alta stopped abruptly. Tears welled up in her eyes. "We ain't got no kind of life with him always drinkin' and losin' his temper." She felt faint, put her face against the cool congo wall next to the kitchen table, and closed her eyes.

Ida Mae wiped her hands on her apron and sat down beside her. She placed her long, slender hand on Alta's shoulder and squeezed it gently.

"I'm goin' to make sure you get to go tomorrow…." She whispered in Alta's ear. "I'll make sure he doesn't know…I ain't puttin' up with him much longer either." She added. "Lord knows, I'm tryin' to get you girls raised up…."

Alta knew her momma was almost at her wit's end with her daddy. She also knew everyone in the family wanted him to quit drinking and be his normal, joking self. But they had long ago realized that the drink had gotten him and, like many miners in the camp, he would never be any different. But this was the first time she had heard her momma say she was going to leave her daddy.

Alta couldn't wait to get her dress ironed and ready. She

chose a black organdy dress that her mother had bought her for her sixteenth birthday. She shined her only pair of patent leather shoes and picked a pretty white bow to wear in her hair. She sorted through her socks and picked a pair without picks or holes. She washed her cotton slip and hung it out to dry on the clothesline strung between the corner post of the chicken lot and the smoke house.

•••

Lance drove his stepside Chevrolet truck up the steep hill to where his mother lived in the small, four-room, wooden-frame coal camp house. The truck backfired as he cut the motor off prematurely, coasted into the graveled drive, and parked behind his 1939 Packard straight-eight sedan. Missouri, his mother, who had been breaking seed heads from her zinnias, jumped, let out a scream, and placed her hand over her heart.

"Lordy, boy. You nearly scared me into tomorrow!" She said. "I don't know, for the life of me, why you want to scare your old mommy that way."

Lance grabbed her around the waist and swung her from her feet in a wide, arching circle. "You ain't never been scared of nothin' but haints and boogermen," he exclaimed as he put her down on the sand rock walkway.

She followed him into the kitchen where there were the smells of hamhocks cooking in beans, cornbread, fried potatoes, and freshly peeled onion. He sat at the yellow metal table, ate three big plates, and finished with two big dollops of butter covered with a wide ribbon of molasses. They turned on the floor model radio and listened to the news.

He went to bed early. For a while, he lay in the feather bed staring at the wooden tongue-and-groove ceiling. He knew what he wanted to do. He wanted to take Alta away from the moonshine whiskey, the hitting, the yelling, the ridiculous late night serenading of drunks.... Suddenly he got up, slipped on his pants and shoes, went out to the smoke house, got the old Samsonite suitcase he had picked up in somebody's garbage pile in the camp, and came back to his room. He opened the dresser drawer and carefully placed two pairs of pleated pants, three white shirts, and four changes of underwear and socks into it. He closed the latches, placed his hands on top of the smooth, brown leather, hefted the case out to the Packard, and placed it in the rear floorboard. He slipped back into the house, got back in the featherbed, and had a fitful night where deep sleep never really came.

•••

Sunday dawned with a golden sun ball cresting over the waves of the mountains. He arose, heated water for a bath in the galvanized tub in the living room and took a quick bath. He shaved by taking the oval mirror from the bedroom wall, placing it on the kitchen table, lathering his face with hand soap, and using his daddy's old straight razor. Halfway through shaving, he cut himself and bled on his undershirt. In his frustration, he wadded it up and threw it into the fireplace. Missouri scolded him for his impatience. He had never been too patient. She had seen him try to stab his feet into his socks and if they didn't go on the first time, he would tear them in half, throw that pair in the corner, and start on another pair.

He drove the big Packard sedan to Machine Shop Hollow, pulled up behind the Car Shop, cut off the motor, and opened the driver's side door. He turned on the radio, lit an Ibold cigar and slowly blew a series of smoke rings and watched them float upward. The faint sounds of the song

"Buttons and Bows" filtered from the radio speaker on the dash: "…let's go where I'll keep wearin'/ Those frills and flowers and buttons and bows/ Rings and things and buttons and bows." The air was crisp and full with the aroma of flowers and leaves wafting out of the hollow.

He heard the faint crunch of her feet on the gravel before she came into sight. He turned his head to watch her come around the corner of the building. She appeared as if some angel had stepped down from heaven and singled him out as he sat in the car. She got in the passenger's side of the front seat, leaned over, kissed him gently on the cheek and began to sing along with the radio as he started the car and they drove toward the center of Black Mountain coal camp. They turned to look at the church, then the clubhouse, and then the road leading out of the camp. She smiled sweetly and snuggled into his shoulder as the muffled voice on the radio sang "I'm all yours in buttons and bows."

ROSES SO RED
by Edwina Pendarvis

It embarrassed Ellen that her forty-year old mother was pregnant. The bigger her mother got, the greater Ellen's embarrassment. By the time her mother was in her ninth month, Ellen could hardly look at her. After the baby was born, she refused to look at him. When her mother called everyone into the bedroom, Ellen hung back.

"Come on," Tom whispered, urging his oldest daughter to join the others as they hurried in to see the baby.

Ellen shook her head, her lips pressed together, a frown on her pretty, freckled face.

Reluctantly, Tom left her standing and followed his younger children through the hall. His wife Jetta lay on the rumpled bed, her graying hair brushed back from her forehead. She looked hot and tired though the birth had been a fairly easy one. Doc Deskins had been there only about an hour.

"It's a boy," she said to the children, as she motioned them to come closer to the infant she held in her arms, "your new brother. Donald, after Uncle Don."

Jetta didn't comment on Ellen's absence. She let the children take turns holding the baby, cautioning them to support its wobbly head. After they had held their new brother, she told them to go back to bed and get some sleep.

The excitement and heat of the August night kept Ellen awake long after the house was quiet. She tried to lie still so she wouldn't disturb her younger sister, Julie, curled up beside her.

Ellen had been more frightened about the birth than she'd known, and now her embarrassment faded as nine-months' worth of worry about her mother rushed over her all at once. She felt sick to her stomach, and the bedroom ceiling seemed to swirl slowly above her head. Closing her eyes, she tried to push away her fears, but couldn't. What if her mother had died? Mrs. Ratliff had died in childbirth just last year. What if the baby died? Ellen lay awake and uncomfortably still for what seemed like hours. Interspersed disturbingly with images of her mother and the baby were images of the handsome young stranger whom she'd heard was the mine supervisor's son. Ellen had seen him only a few times, but couldn't stop thinking about him. Finally she fell asleep. When she woke, tears had gathered under her closed eyelids. She opened her eyes. It wasn't daylight yet.

As she lay awake in the dark, an old memory came to mind: a scene from seven years ago—it was mid-November and spitting snow. Ellen's Grandpa Johnson and her mother, far along in her sixth pregnancy, were butchering a hog. Tom was at work in Pikeville, and wouldn't be home until the weekend, so Jetta helped her father in-law with the heavy work. Clumsily, she struggled to help scald the dead hog with boiling water and scrape it after they'd hung the heavy carcass from its hind legs so the blood would drain out of the slit in its throat. The next day, her labor started, and her sixth child, Bennett, was born, nearly a month early. For a few days, they weren't sure the baby would survive.

When Ellen woke next, the morning sun shone brightly through the curtains.

"Get up!" Julie whispered. She'd been leaning over her sister, whiling away the time tracing with her finger the entwined flowers stamped into the metal headboard of their bed; but she couldn't wait any longer. As soon as Ellen opened her eyes, the younger girl bounced off the bed, wide awake and eager to do all the housework her mother usually did. Her skinny arms and legs stuck out of her undershirt and panties like knobby sticks. Ellen propped herself on her elbows and looked sleepily at her little sister, then across the room at her younger brothers—Paul, Fon, and J.O., sound asleep on the other bed, and Bennett, on the cot. From the other bedroom the baby cried, sounding so indignant that both girls smiled. Ellen felt a pang of guilt at her inability to look at the baby, but she could not bring herself to walk into her parents' room. She pulled on a short-sleeved cotton dress and combed her hair as Julie ran to tell her mother and the baby good morning.

Jetta, nursing the infant, closed her gown as Julie walked into the room.

"Just give him a kiss and go on, honey. He's hungry," Jetta said.

Julie bent over the bed and kissed the baby on the top of its fuzzy head. She touched his tiny hand lightly to feel its smooth newness, then hurried out of the room to get dressed.

Ellen lit the kindling in the blue enamel cookstove and told Julie to start the biscuits. Only after the younger girl accidentally sifted flour onto the linoleum, would she let Ellen steady the sifter for her, holding it over the big yellow mixing bowl. Ellen poured buttermilk into the flour, baking powder, soda, and lard then let her sister knead the dough.

Fourteen-year-old Paul was the first of the boys to awaken. He walked into the kitchen, his hair sticking up, ruffled from sleep. He had pulled on his trousers, but was still barefoot and bare-chested. His lanky frame made the kitchen look smaller. He walked over to the table and sat down.

"Any coffee?" he asked.

"I didn't fix any," Ellen answered, handing him a glass. He picked up the pitcher of milk and poured himself a full glass.

"You're going to hurt Mama's feelings," Paul warned his older sister as she sliced strips of bacon from a slab of meat.

"She oughtn't to have a baby at her age," Ellen said, uncomfortable at being confronted openly. She didn't know what to say. It seemed near blasphemy to speak critically of their mother, whom all six brothers and sisters held more dear than anything else.

Troubled by this rupture in their accord, the two were quiet, and for a few minutes the sounds of bacon sizzling and the bustle of breakfast preparations took the place of conversation. Ellen busied herself turning the bacon, lifting it out of the pan, and pouring flour into the bubbling grease to make gravy.

After a few minutes, Bennett hurried into the kitchen as though he were late for something.

"Breakfast isn't ready. You'll just have to wait," Julie informed him in her five-year-old's imitation of an admonishing tone.

Outside, the sounds of women calling to each other as they swept the front steps or hung out clothes filled the morning air. Most of the men had been at work since before daylight drilling into a wall of coal, working it with pickaxes, shoveling the coal and loading it into trams to be hauled out of the mine. Tom had been at the company store for hours. Glancing out the window as she put food on the table, Ellen could see past the houses almost to the river with its leafy awning of water birches. The thought of the sparkling, sun-lit water and the sight of the green trees brought her a sense of relief from the heat of the kitchen and from the remnants of her fears of the night before.

Fon, fully dressed, his hair neatly combed, walked in and stood in the middle of the kitchen. Ellen motioned for him to sit down as she carried the skillet to the table and spooned some gravy onto his plate.

"Go wake J.O.," she told Bennett.

After breakfast, Ellen let Julie stand up on a chair in front of the sink to help wash dishes. All day they did the work their mother usually did—sweeping the kitchen, making beds, and washing clothes in the new washer with rollers that squeezed the soapy water out of their laundry. Paul had to go help their father at the store, but the younger boys fed the chickens, weeded the garden, and brought in coal for the cookstove. All day Fon, J.O., Bennett, and Julie took turns checking on their mother and the new baby.

When Paul and Tom got home from work, Tom told the children since they'd worked hard all day, they could go over to the store and listen to the radio after supper dishes were done. "Grand Ole Opry,"one of the town's favorites, was on tonight. There'd be lots of people at the store.

It was still daylight and still hot when the brothers and sisters walked into the store together. Ellen and Julie urged their brothers to sit down on the floor next to them, leaning against the glassed-in candy counter on which the Philco radio sat. The boys wanted to sit nearer to the door, though, so they could slip out and sit on the front steps with any of their friends who came by. After about half an hour, Julie got sleepy and lay down, putting her head in Ellen's lap. Ellen stroked her little sister's shiny black hair, smoothing it away from her face while they listened to jokes and country music that had traveled all the way from Nashville, Tennessee, to this little town of forty miners and their families in Kentucky's eastern highlands. A feeling of drowsy contentment washed through Ellen as she looked around the store at her neighbors and family. She pictured her mother and baby brother sleeping only a few houses away. Surrounding the houses, she felt the sheltering mountains. Though she sometimes missed the farm they'd lived on till a few years ago, tonight she felt glad to be in Dunleary Hollow.

As the strains of "Wildwood Flower" filled the room, Ellen noticed her brothers get up and step into the twilight outside the store. She heard the boys calling to one another as they started a game of tag. Teenage couples drifted in and out of the evening shadows that hid their whispers and kisses. The music inside and voices outside blended together into a harmony that made Ellen feel strange, both happy and sad without knowing why. When it was time to go home, Tom picked Julie up and carried her, still sleeping, in his arms. Ellen called to the boys to come on and hurried to keep pace with Tom's long stride. When she went to bed she slept soundly, waking only occasionally to familiar noises—frogs croaking down by the river, a train whistle in the night.

Next morning, after the boys had scattered to play, Ellen picked up two buckets and left the house to go to the pump in the middle of town. At the farm, she'd enjoyed going to the creek to get water. She could wade in the creek hunting for salamanders. The clear water was like a window through which she could see pretty rocks or the slow motion of a crawdad easing across the sand floor and its sudden backward dart under a stone. As she pushed down on the pump handle, she remembered the smell of mint growing alongside the creek on their old farm.

On her way home with the water, just as she passed the pony shed, Ellen heard the buzz of a small plane overhead. She thought it must be Dave Chapman's plane and squinted up at the glint of silver, then looked toward the Chapman's house. Sure enough, there lay the orange sheet Mrs. Chapman spread out on the ground every time she knew her son would be flying over.

George Chapman, the mine supervisor, and his wife Nina had moved to Dunleary from Cincinnati. Although Ellen had never been inside their house, she'd heard it was furnished like no other house in the hollow. The miners who'd moved the furniture in told their wives the Chapmans had brought a piano, real oil paintings, and crystal drinking-glasses. Mrs. Chapman sometimes came down the hill to visit Ellen's mother, though she always came alone; her husband didn't socialize much with employees or their families. Once, Mrs. Chapman had given Jetta a beautiful umbrella stand with irises painted on it for helping her crochet a bedspread.

Ellen thought the Chapmans' son was the handsomest man she'd ever seen. His black eyebrows and long, black eyelashes contrasted sharply with his blonde hair and blue eyes. She envied him the tawny color of his skin. She wondered how old he was and guessed him to be about twenty.

In her reverie, she forgot the heavy water buckets she was carrying. Then she remembered the time a few weeks ago when Dave Chapman had tried to talk to her.

The young man had called hello from his yard as Ellen walked by on her way to the swimming hole. Turning around,

she'd been surprised to see the mine supervisor's son leaning against a fence post. Ellen ducked her head. She quickened her step and walked by him as fast as she could, but she
felt the heat rising from her neck to her cheeks and knew
she must be blushing a bright red. When she heard a quiet
laugh behind her, she thought she would cry from shame.

This jarring memory brought Ellen back to the present,
and she put the buckets down for a moment to flex her sore
hands before picking the pails back up and continuing home.

Ellen went about the rest of her morning chores thinking
of Dave, torn between wishing their embarrassing meeting
had never happened and being pleased he had spoken to her.
That afternoon when her mother asked her to go to the
store for some evaporated milk, she walked absent-
mindedly, still daydreaming, enjoying the rustle of the
wind high in the trees and looking up occasionally at the
deep blue August sky. She could feel autumn in the air
though the day was still hot enough for her to welcome the
cool dimness of the store when she stepped inside. Just as
she started to speak to her father, standing at the counter,
she heard footsteps behind her.

"Dave, good to see you," her father said, speaking past
Ellen to the youth who had walked into the store just after
she did.

"Mr. Johnson, it's been a while. How've you been?" Dave
asked, reaching out to shake Tom's hand.

"Just fine," Tom replied.

Dave looked at Ellen.

"This is Ellen, my oldest," Tom said.

"Hi, Ellen" said Dave.

"Nice meeting you," Ellen managed to say in a voice barely
above a whisper. Not sure whether her father would think

her rude if she walked away to get the milk, she stood there.

"I saw you on your way to swim last time I was here," Dave said to her, "Are you going this afternoon?"

"No," Ellen answered quickly, "I've got work to do at home."

"Maybe I'll see you there tomorrow then," Dave said, handing Ellen's father some change for a pack of cigarettes, "See you later, Mr. Johnson."

Tom wrote down the price for the cans of milk on his charge account and told Ellen she could go swimming with her brother Paul tomorrow if she wanted. Ellen thanked him and then took her time leaving the store, so she'd not catch up to Dave. A few yards ahead of her, however, the young man stooped down, then stood up and turned around.

"A four-leaf clover," he said. "It's a lucky sign; it means I should walk you home—if you don't mind."

Ellen took the clover he held out to her, and he took the paper bag she carried. As he walked beside her, he pretended not to notice her shyness and asked questions about the town and about the garden next to the Johnson house. Ellen was surprised to learn he couldn't tell sweet-potato vines from squash vines. She relaxed a little as she pointed out the different plants, and even smiled when he complimented her on the roses she'd planted in front of the house. The velvety red blossoms bloomed full-blown, almost too heavy for the slender twigs that held them. When the couple reached the doorstep, Dave returned the bag to her, and said he wished she'd meet him at the swimming hole tomorrow. That night, she dreamed about him and woke up at dawn excited at the prospect of seeing him again.

After their chores were finished that afternoon, she and Paul walked down the river bank to the swimming hole. Ellen tugged at her suit every few steps. Always self-conscious about being thin, she felt exposed in her modest, silvery green bathing suit. Looking down at her legs, she wished they were curvier. She wished she weren't so pale. She wished Dave wouldn't show up, but hoped he would. Paul, always serious, could be counted on not to tease her about her new "boyfriend." He walked through the weeds a little in front of her, holding bushes aside as he passed so branches wouldn't fly back and hit her. They could hear kids yelling and splashing before they could see them. Then, just before they reached the riverbank, Ellen saw Dave swinging far out over the river on the big vine they all used to launch themselves into the air. At the top of the vine's arc he dropped through the sunlight into the water.

Friends called to the brother and sister as they walked down the steep bank and onto the sandy shore. Ellen greeted the cheerful, boisterous youngsters and hung her towel over a fallen sycamore. Carefully avoiding looking toward the middle of the river where Dave might be, she walked to the edge of the water and waded in. When the cold water reached her knees, she raised her hands above her head and gave a little jump, diving into the lazy current. She swam underwater, exhilarated by the feeling of buoyancy and fluid resistance against her movement. Her graceful arms and legs flashed, almost iridescent, just under the surface of the water. A strong swimmer, Ellen felt at home in the water even though she didn't get to swim very often.

When at last she raised her head to get her breath, she looked across the ripples straight into the eyes she'd been avoiding. Dave struck out toward her, his blonde hair in wet spikes against his temples. Ellen treaded water, waiting for him. At his approach she shivered, more from nervousness than from a chill. Half wanting to escape, she looked wistfully toward the little isle in the middle of the river. With birds flitting through the trees on its shore, the sandbar seemed to beckon refuge. Dave swam up alongside her, noticing the direction of her glance.

"Let's swim over there. Want to race?"

As good a swimmer as he was, Dave had to admire Ellen's skill. She moved through the water easily, each stroke of her arm and kick of her leg giving her the most possible distance for her size. Although he moved ahead at the beginning of their race, he could see that if they had farther to swim, he'd have a hard time beating her. His height and strength gave him enough of an advantage to win in this short distance, but when they got to shallow water, he stood up beside her, took one of her hands and held it up.

"The winner!" he announced to the birds flying above, then lowered her hand still holding it.

"I'm not," she demurred and drew her hand away. A shadow of disappointment crossed his face. For a moment both of them stood not knowing what to say, the jar-flies' chirrup ringing in their ears. Ellen could feel minnows nibbling at her toes under the waist-deep water. She wished she could think of something to say, but all she could do was stand there, keenly aware of Dave's presence beside her.

She was almost relieved when Ballard Newsome swam up and asked if they wanted to join a game of banner man. He explained the game to Dave, telling him it was a game of follow-the-leader; followers had to attempt any stunt demonstrated by the banner man. Dave told Ballard to go on without them; they'd join the game later maybe. He and Ellen waded to the sandbar and sat down in the shade. Across the river, on the far side of the coal camp, a C& O engine billowed steam as it chugged away from the tipple, trailing gondolas of blue-black coal. Dave asked the dark-haired young girl if she'd ever been away from home.

"What's the farthest you've ever traveled," he asked.

"I've been to Cincinnati," she said, "on the excursion train. I went with my cousins this summer. The train was mostly taking people to see a Reds ballgame, but we went to the zoo. What's the farthest you've ever been?"

"Last year I flew to Miami, Florida."

"Don't you get scared when you're flying?"

"Sometimes," he answered, smiling at the intenseness of her gaze as she looked directly into his eyes for the first time since they'd met.

"I don't understand how planes fly," she admitted reluctantly. "I mean, we studied it in science…. Of course, I know it's different from a bird. One time I saw a picture of a plane with wings that flapped. It didn't fly, at least not far."

"Yeah, too much energy would be needed to flap big wings hard enough and fast enough. A light plane could glide a long way once it was up in the air, even without a propeller; but to go wherever you want regardless of the winds and to get there fast, you need the propeller, and the propeller needs a motor.

"It sounds reasonable, but it seems impossible. It's hard to believe anything heavier than dust could float through something as light as air."

She looked up at the birds gliding and dipping in the sky above.

"My little sister Julie would say a bird's heart is its motor," she said, liking the image of a red heart, blooming like a flower, inside the breast of each of the little creatures flying above them.

Dave leaned closer to her, looking into her eyes, and to Ellen his gray-blue eyes looked exactly the color of the sky. Suddenly, Ellen felt an impulse to put her hand against Dave's chest to feel the sun-warmed skin above his heart. He leaned closer and kissed her lightly on the lips then quickly pulled away. He put his arm around her waist and said something to her, but she was so flustered she couldn't hear him. She was afraid the others had seen, she was afraid he was so bold because she was just a girl from a coal camp, she was afraid she would fall in love with someone who wouldn't love her; but in spite of her fears, she wanted to feel his lips on hers again.

Dave had been apologizing for almost a minute by the time what he was saying registered. He told Ellen he'd not meant to do that and hoped she wasn't angry with him. He asked her to come over and have dinner at his parents' house tomorrow night and afterward go to a movie in Pikeville.

Ellen knew she'd have to cook dinner for her family, so she asked him if he wanted to meet her at the store instead and listen to the radio or go for a walk.

"I'd like that," he said and stood up, holding out his hand to help her up.

"Come on, you two," yelled someone from the rocks on the bank. "Let's see what kind of nerve you got. Ballard's still banner man."

Ellen and Dave waded into the water, dived in, and swam toward the others.

"You have to hold your breath underwater as long as Ballard does," one of the boys called as they came up to the group. Everyone was looking out toward the middle of the river.

"Ninety-five seconds, so far," Ballard's best friend, Gary,

said, counting out loud slowly.

Soon Ballard burst out of the water, almost leaping up, gasping for breath.

"Let's see if you can beat that!" he exclaimed when he got his breath back.

"Not me," Gary's girlfriend, Betty, said. "I'm not even going to try." Most of the other girls nodded in agreement and waded back to the bank to sit and look on. Ellen stayed in the water, standing between Dave and her brother.

"I'll try it," Paul said. Like Ellen, he prided himself on his swimming. Though he was one of the youngest in the group, he often beat the older boys in races.

Paul's long, skinny arms churned through the water toward the spot where Ballard had been. When he reached the middle of the river, he turned toward the others, waved, held his nose, and submerged.

Gary began to count. As he counted, Dave and Ellen looked out over the river toward the place Paul had ducked underwater. Ballard headed to where the girls sat and ran as fast as he could, splashing water on them as he ran. They jumped up, protesting and giggling at the same time, backing away from the rowdy youngster. The commotion caused Gary to turn around, too, and his girlfriend called to him laughingly

"Gary, help! Make Ballard stop!"

"Just a minute, Judy" Gary called back. "Ballard, stop it! What number are we on? Seventy-something?"

"Seventy-eight," Dave said.

"He's doing good," said Ellen.

"Seventy-nine, eighty," Gary continued counting.

"Gary!" Judy called again as he reached ninety-three.

"Shoot," Gary exclaimed, and turned to Dave, "would you

count? I'm going to give Ballard what's coming to him."

"It's about ninety-six, I think," said Ellen.

"Ninety-seven," Dave went on, "ninety-eight, ninety-nine, one hundred...."

A movement, barely discernible under the water where Paul was, caught Ellen's attention. Something was wrong. Suddenly, it seemed like a long time since her brother went under. Without a word, she started swimming fast toward her brother. As she swam, she thought of all the things that could have happened. Surely he hadn't gotten tangled; there wasn't anything but mud under the river out there in the middle. Maybe he had a cramp. He's all right, she said to herself; he's just being stubborn, just being Paul, intense about everything, determined to win. Still, she tried to swim faster. As she got nearer, she put her head underwater and opened her eyes. She thought she could make him out dimly through the water. As she got closer, her alarm grew. His body looked lax. Now almost to him, she saw with horror his mouth gaping open. She swam under him and shoved his trunk upward, trying to push his head up out of the water. Then she grabbed him from behind, her right arm encircling his neck, and gave a powerful kick starting back with him. She struggled through the water only a few seconds before Dave arrived to help support the unconscious boy and get him back on the riverbank. By now, Ballard, Gary, and two other boys were swimming out to meet them. The girls stood huddled in shallow water, looking scared.

Dave, Gary, and Ballard laid Paul on his stomach on the sand.

"Put his hands over his head," one of the girls said. Ellen knelt over Paul and took hold of one of his unresisting hands and then the other, lifting his arms gently, and placing them with his palms down, in the position a picture in their health book had shown for resuscitating victims of drowning. Ballard moved her aside.

"Let me. I'm stronger," he said, and began pressing down on Paul's back.

Dave took hold of Paul's wrist and felt for a pulse. His frown brought tears to Ellen's eyes, and she started to cry. Betty put her arm around Ellen.

"Wait," Dave said. "I can't tell—somebody else feel." Ballard was sweating now, afraid of pushing too hard on the boy's thin back and afraid of not pushing hard enough. Water trickled out of Paul's mouth and nose.

Ellen looked at Gary.

"Go get somebody to help," the distraught girl pleaded.

Gary turned to run when a strangled noise stopped him.

Ellen bent down close to her brother, whispering his name.

Paul coughed while the others patted and poked him, reassuring him and each other that he was okay. He raised up on his elbows, too weak to say anything.

"I guess he showed you," Gary teased Ballard. Ellen couldn't even smile. She sat down beside Paul, and Dave sat down not far away.

While they waited for the boy to recover, the teenagers talked quietly, laughing occasionally, their nervousness fading. At last, Paul stood up.

"We'd better go home," Ellen said. Dave walked with them. They waved good-bye to their friends and started up the bank, Dave behind in case Paul needed help up the steep incline.

At home that evening, after her parents had fussed over Paul, after Dave had gone home, and her brothers and sister were asleep, Ellen lay on the bed in her parents' room, trying to read. Distracted by chaotic memories of the day, she glanced up from her magazine and noticed her reflection in the big mirror hanging on the bedroom wall. The baby lay in his bassinet just under and to the side of the mirror. Ellen got up and looked surreptitiously into the mirror at the reflection of his tiny face. She turned her eyes away quickly when she heard her mother's voice.

"It's about time," Jetta said as she walked into the bedroom, letting her daughter know she'd seen the covert look. Ellen said nothing but, a few seconds later she walked up to the side of the bassinet and took her first good look at her youngest brother. She picked him up and held him close.

THE LEGEND OF ARACOMA
by Laura Treacy Bentley

Boling Baker lets the current take him. Holding onto the
raft, he imagines a watery death. It seems painless compared
to a tortured death by the Shawnee or the French. He watches
the shoreline slide by. A stag appears from the woods to
drink. A turtle surfaces. Crows call from the woods. The
Ohio River carries him away from a bloody war. A deserter.
Not the first nor the last, but still a deserter. Better that, than
sure death in a war this British soldier did not understand.

Two miles down? Ten? How far will the Ohio carry him?
In the smoky dusk, distance is washed away. The current takes
him near the shore; his path is slowed by thick brush at the
confluence of the Ohio and Kanawha rivers. He lets go of
the raft and swims closer, his arms like iron weights in
the cold water. Baker commands his worn body toward
land. He reaches for exposed tree roots and pulls himself
onto a silty shore. Crawling on his stomach until he
reaches dry land, he falls asleep exhausted among creeper
and scrub pine. Ten, twelve, fourteen hours, and when he
wakes it is light. He raises his head and is surrounded by
Shawnee. They bind his hands and ankles in silence and carry
him to their village where they lay him at the feet of

Hokolesqua, Chief Cornstalk, sachem of the Shawnee.

Chief Cornstalk is tired of the warring and the anti-Indian British, tired of fighting for what is already his. Cornstalk had wanted to remain neutral in the white man's war; but he believes what Chiksika said: "The white race is a monster who is always hungry, and what he eats is land."

Baker lies stunned. Although it is hot, he shivers violently in his wet clothes. His feet are bare, boots and socks somewhere at the bottom of the Ohio river. Cornstalk—remembering how the British gave smallpox-infested blankets to the Shawnee and Delaware when they came to discuss peace, how the scourge passed from village to village, how this British "Peace" poisoned his people—signals death for his enemy captive. The warriors seize him once more.

Aracoma, daughter of Chief Cornstalk, is sixteen summers. She watches the white man at her father's feet and studies his features: his eyes the color of the sky, the fear on his handsome face. Aracoma named for the corn blossom, the first flower her mother saw after her daughter was born, falls to her knees and asks her father to spare the life of this white man from the river. Chief Cornstalk looks at his beautiful daughter, and then he looks out over his land and his people. He nods to Aracoma, and the warriors release Baker. Aracoma smiles and looks into the soldier's blue eyes.

In time, Baker becomes Shawnee and much loved by Cornstalk, whose words must have echoed those of Black Fish when Daniel Boone was adopted into the tribe:

> My son, you are now flesh of our flesh and bone of our bone. By the ceremony performed this day, every drop of white blood was washed from your veins; you were taken into the Shawnee nation...you were adopted into a great family.

Baker hunts for deer and wild turkey in the eastern mountains with his adopted tribe, sleeps under the stars in summer, and falls deeply in love with Aracoma.

When the day comes for the ceremony to make Aracoma a tribal leader, neighboring tribes travel to Cornstalk's village. Oceana, Aracoma's sister, and the other women build a large fire; the men begin to chant in a steady rhythm to the beat of drums and gourd rattles. Soon the men begin to dance in a circle; Baker moves and turns his body in time to the drums as if he were born Shawnee. The women gradually join in, choosing a partner as they enter the dance. Aracoma in beaded and quilled deerskin and painted ceremonial robe begins to dance. Her eyes fall on the blue-eyed warrior, and she chooses him as her partner. The soft shuffle of moccasins and the shadows of feather and fringe call forth the blessing of the Mother Spirit while proud Chief Cornstalk watches over his daughter and his adopted son.

The feasting lasts until dawn. Buffalo, deer, and turkey are roasted, and parched corn, blackberries, persimmons, and paw-paws are placed in wooden bowls. Cornstalk calls Aracoma to him, blesses her, and places two eagle feathers in her hand: "For courage and vision, my daughter."

Chief Cornstalk assigns Aracoma a tribe to lead, and she sends two scouts to find a new home. After many months, they return with news that her promised land is found. Giving the scouts time to rest and readying her tribe for the long march, Aracoma announces to all the chiefs of the neighboring tribes who gather to say farewell, that she will marry the white man in three months. This news is immediately accepted and celebrated that night, only to cease so the travelers will have a few hours of much needed sleep before their journey.

With the scouts in the lead, Aracoma, her future husband, and her new tribe follow the Kanawha River for days. The small band is spread out for miles, as the young and the old carry their belongings to the new land. Aracoma is no stranger to migration; it is the way of life for the Shawnee. After building many campfires, crossing rivers, and mountain ranges, they see their new hunting grounds in the distance. As the sun is setting, the tribe reaches the banks of the Guyan River, crosses a stream, and settles on a small island in the middle of a rushing river. There Aracoma and her people build permanent dwellings in a circle—oblong lodges with pitched roofs. They cover them carefully with bark from the birch and elm. The men make canoes, and the women plant yellow, red, blue, and white corn. Bean, pumpkin, squash, and sunflower seeds are sown; soon tobacco sprouts in the rich earth.

A few weeks later, in preparation for Aracoma's wedding, runners are dispatched to tell Chief Cornstalk that the time for the wedding is near. Once again, preparations are made. Fish are caught in great numbers, and the choicest cuts of venison are prepared. Many chiefs and their tribes arrive for the ceremony that lasts three days. On the second evening, Aracoma steps forth from the largest lodge to wed Boling Baker. Under a full moon, the tribe forms a huge circle around the couple, and Chief Cornstalk speaks the words that unite them forever.

On the island surrounded by the Guyan River, their first year together passes happily. Aracoma gives birth to their first child, a son. Naming him after the first thing she sees following his birth, she calls him Waulalapa, Laughing Waters, after the rippling stream. In time, Aracoma gives birth to Snow Lily, Raindrop, Running Deer, and Blue Feather. Each morning, summer or winter, she bathes her children in the cold waters of the Guyan River to make them strong.

A snake slithers into Aracoma's paradise in the form of a plague, a plague brought by the white men which begins to destroy her people since they have no protection against the white man's diseases. One by one the young and the old take sick and die; the survivors are weak and hungry. Curative roots and herbs cannot fight this terrible disease. Even the shaman's prayers cannot suck this evil from their bodies. Aracoma and Baker hold fast to each other as one by one their own children die and are taken across the "laughing waters" stream and buried with their faces turned toward the setting sun. Aracoma is sick with grief. Afraid they are cursed, the tribe threatens to leave the island and journey to a new land.

Desperate, Baker conspires to travel east to white settlements on the Bluestone River, to get help for the tribe any way he can, even if it means treachery against his own kind. Settlers take him in out of pity for the white man captured by savages. They cut his hair and give him decent clothes to wear. After one month, Baker betrays their trust, steals their horses, and returns to Aracoma.

With guns and knives, ninety men under the command of General Madison, follow moccasin tracks back to the village. Aracoma's people are hunted and killed for fifty horses; ten lodges are burned and destroyed. The white men search the faces of the dead and dying for the face of their betrayer: Boling Baker.

Now Aracoma is running, running for her life, but a shot rings out. She lies mortally wounded. "My husband," she cries out in Shawnee, but Baker has escaped into a lost river.

Aracoma touches the hand of her captor and says:

> My name is Aracoma, and I am the last of a mighty race. My father was a great chief and a friend of your people. He was murdered in cold blood by the whites when he came to them as a friend to give them a warning. I am the wife of a paleface who came across the great waters to make war on my people but came to us and was made one of us. A great plague many moons ago carried off my children, and they were buried just above the bend in the river. Bury me with them with my face toward the setting sun, that I may see my people on their march to the next world.

Aracoma makes it through the long night, but when the sun begins to rise she takes her last breath. The settlers moved by her plight, do as she asks. They wrap her slender body in deerskin and bury her with her children in an unmarked grave.

Legend has it that an old man with a British accent came there years later looking for Aracoma's burial ground. After it was shown to him, he was given a place to stay for the night and died in his sleep. Some say it was Boling Baker, the man from the river, the man with eyes the color of sky, come back to sleep forever in the arms of his beautiful wife.

JAMES ALEXANDER MOORE
by James M. Gifford

For more than a century, chroniclers have regaled their readers with the physical and political impact of America's Civil War. Now that the rift in union is finally being mended, Northerners and Southerners (and those war-enforced regional distinctions will never die) are finally reconstructing a war-torn nation. Unfortunately, scholars have too often emphasized the war's effect on later generations of Americans. An occasional reflection on the misery of the 1860s may result in a more realistic assessment by those who glorify the war and deify its participants. The brief diary kept by James Alexander Moore, who eventually ascended to the captain's rank in the Forty-first Tennessee Infantry Regiment, provides clear insight to war-imposed trauma and offers sad commentary on the emotional drain and the daily uncertainties—the soldier's universal malaise—endured by "The Bedford County Guards."

James Alexander Moore was born in Shelbyville, Bedford County, Tennessee, although his exact birthdate is unknown. Like most antebellum Americans, the Moores went to their fields and beds in peace—not oblivious to the tumultuous events that shattered the national scene with increasing regularity, but not greatly affected by them either. Late in the 1850s, James entered the famous Cumberland Law School at Lebanon, Tennessee. He graduated in 1861, just as the quiet rhythmic cadence of American life quickened to the beat of the drums of war.

Moore soon joined Company "K" of the Forty-first Tennessee Infantry Regiment. He left for the war on the last day of October, 1861. Less than four months later, his regiment was defeated at the battle of Fort Donelson (Tennessee). The entire command, companies A-K, surrendered February 16, 1862. Moore was then transported to a Union P.O.W. camp, Camp Chase, in Columbus, Ohio. A month before his capture, Moore penned the following letter to his parents:

Camp Buckner Near Bowling Green,
Sunday evening Jan 19th, 1862

Man's life is as fleeting as the breeze that fans us. Like unto the flower that sheds its sweetness in all its native beauty, in one short hour it droops—it pines—it dies. Like the beautiful star at evening twilight that shines forth in all its brillancy and heavenly splendor, it sits in blackest night, or is lost in the more perfect splendor of early dawn. So with man. Vanity is his food of life. He lives today in the strength of man-hood—in one short week the grass grows upon his grave. Heaven prepare us for the awful change that awaits us. We are now in an enemy's land away from our homes and those we love. We stand as it were, upon a mighty precipice. In the distance are flowers of every hue, with a narrow and dangerous path leading thereto. One step to the right or the left and all is lost. If successful, we may ramble amidst the flowers and bind the wreath of fame. But who is to live to gather the flowers? God only knows. My last will is, if I never return I want my father and mother ever to treat Mattie Jones as a daughter, and my brothers and sisters to treat her as a sister. For she is to be my bride. Love her for my sake, and treat her with every kindness. When you get this send for her and read this to her and welcome her to every hospitality that you do the rest of your children. This is the last will of your son

James A. Moore

Lingering near death, Moore was released from Camp Chase to the care of a local widow, one Mrs. Newcomb, and her two daughters, Hattie and Nellie. Their kind attentions saved his life. When his health had partially returned, Moore signed a parole, by which he agreed to "do no act of hostility, nor either speak nor write against, nor furnish any aid or information to the Enemies of the government of the United States."

Moore returned to Shelbyville and eventually married Mattie A. Jones on August 20, 1863. He began a successful law practice. However, he never completely recovered from his war-time illnesses. He died on March 31, 1872. Like so many, he was a casualty of the war.

OLD PAP'S STORY: AN ORAL HISTORY
by Bruce Radford Richey

I grew up in Monroe County, Kentucky, near Tompkinsville in a beautiful old home built by my great grand-father, (Old Pap) Preston Richey. Old Pap left on horseback in 1863 to fight the Union Army. He had started building the house in 1860. He had it all done except for the fireplaces that stood on each end. They were half way complete when Old Pap left for the war. Old Pap was so in love with his new bride, Eleanor, (Old Ma).This was to be his greatest present to her—a new home where they could raise a family and live and farm for the rest of their lives.

Old Pap did not get to return until the end of the war. In August, 1865, he walked from Big Stone Gap, Virginia, to Mt. Hermon, Kentucky. About two months before he arrived home, Union troops had marched through the area, doing all they could to harm the people of the area who were Southern sympathizers.

One day about twenty of them came to my house. They asked my grandmother to fix them something to eat. She must have been fearless, for she told them to go elsewhere and fix their own food. Reacting to these words, they raped her and then blinded her. From then on, she refused to leave the house for fear she would miss Old Pap. She hired a black lady, Miss Louise, to take care of her.

When Old Pap got home (as the story was told and retold in my family), he looked at the house from the hilltop, and watched to see if he could set eyes on his beautiful new bride that he had not seen in over two years. But alas all he could see was Miss Louise hanging out clothes. He left the site where he was sitting, and cleaned up in the cold water of the creek, because he wanted to look good for his wife. He made his way down to the house and asked Miss Louise where Eleanor was. Grimly Miss Louise said she was in the house. He rushed in and saw her sitting way up on the stairway in a dark corner. He rushed to her and with all the kindness in the world hugged her and kissed her, over and over. The corner was very dark and he was wonderfully happy, so he picked her up and carried her to the upstairs bedroom and there in the light found her to be blind.

He went a little mad after he found out what had happened. Days turned to months, months turned to years, and he worked and worked. First to finish the house, then the farm, and finally the 600 acres that was his part of the Richey farm. He did everything he could to see that Old Ma was at ease because he loved her with undying love. Ma was so beautiful. She had dark, brown eyes and skin the color of the light brown earth in that part of the country. He would read to her, take her on walks, tell her of his plants and harvest, tell her how the house looked. At the top of the fireplaces he finished, he inscribed, "For Eleanor," a monument to his love that stands today.

Old Ma died in 1911 at the age of 86. She is buried in the Little Richey Grave Yard on our family farm. After her death, Old Pa became even more disturbed— "crazy" some would call it. After the funeral, he moved out of the house they had built, the loving place where they had raised their children. He turned it over to my grandfather, Jimmy Richey. Then Old Pap, wandered around from place to place, camped outdoors and grew a long beard. He was often seen with his rifle and with rabbits hanging from his belt. He, I believe, was not crazy, only sad. After six years of wandering, he could no longer stand being away from Eleanor. So he built a lean-to beside her grave, and that is where he lived the balance of his life. They say he would talk to her as if she was alive, build a fire at early night, eat his catch of the day and drink his coffee. If anyone came around he would tell them to leave. "Just let me be," he would say.

One day my grandfather went to check on him and found him dead under the old lean-to. In his hand was dirt he had pulled away from Old Ma's grave. They said that in his dying moments he must have been trying to dig down to her. I often wonder what his last thoughts were.

I go back there, from time to time, to visit and there they are, side by side, and as if almost by magic the old cedar trees seem to tell me of their love and remind me of my youth and my love for the house. The place where Old Pap found Old Ma was always called "Old Ma's corner" and it was a spooky place. I felt a chill each time I went by there. Later, as a teenager, I got up the nerve to see what was there and found an old trunk, filled with books and papers from the war. I touched Old Ma's clothes and belongings and felt something magical. It was love I was feeling, the love of Preston and Eleanor Richey.

HELPFUL ROMANTICS
by Ina Everman

My dad didn't like the fellow I was engaged to for a number of reasons. One evening, right before going to bed, Daddy knocked at my door and said, "Can we talk?"

"Sure, Dad, come on in. What's the problem?" His brow was more furrowed than usual and his green eyes were turning gray.

"I know that you think you're in love with Rich, but…. there's just somethin' a gnawin' at me. For some reason I just don't feel good about you marryin' him." He flatly stated his reasons why he felt Rich was not the man for me. The biggest was Rich's lack of faith and commitment to the Lord and to church. "Here's a deal…. You and me are gonna pray together for six weeks. We're gonna pray especially for God to send you the right man. If no new man comes along—then I'll give you my blessing. BUT…."

I agreed and for the next two weeks, we prayed every night. On the second Saturday, after we started, Rich and I had a major disagreement and he left me standing on a street corner downtown. Not five minutes after he pulled away, Ted pulled up, asked if I needed a ride, and through the tears, I sniffled, "Yeah, thanks." It was Memorial Day weekend.

I had known Ted almost all my life. We grew up together in the local church and were friends, even though he was five years my senior. My parents and his were friends, my mother and his were in the same Sunday School class. Daddy was tickled to death when I told him that on the way home Ted had asked me to go out to eat and to see a movie.

Saturday evening came and Ted picked me up at 6:30. Not one to talk a lot, Ted kept rather still on the way to the restaurant. Feeling very uncomfortable with every moment of silence, I chattered all the way. Eating at the steak house was better because it's not polite to talk with your mouth full. I guess I gave his ears a little break. We went to see "2001: A Space Odyssey." We missed the first ten minutes and the entire point of the film. Boring!

The drive home was exactly like the drive to the steak house. I talked and he muttered now and then. We parked in front of my house and he actually walked me to the door, something Rich rarely did.

Daddy was anxiously waiting in the living room. "Well...how was it? Do you like him? Where did you go? He's a good fellow, isn't he?' The barrage went on. Trying not to be rude, I just listened and nodded my head.

The night had been so boring and I had felt so uncomfortable, I didn't care what Daddy thought. I never gave the "Deal" a thought either. The only thing I could stammer was, "Be my luck I'll marry a jerk like that."

I learned later, Ted had gone home and told his mother, "That gal talks more than all five of my sisters put together."

Within the next week, Rich and I had had another fight and I had broken the engagement. Whining to my Dad didn't work. "I just don't know what to do. What do I tell people? I thought he loved me, Daddy."

Putting his arm around my shoulders and smirking, he calmly stated, "You don't need Rich, he's not the right guy for you. Have you forgotten…God sent you Ted!"

"Ted! That bore! You really believe he's the answer to our prayers?"

"Honey, where's your faith? God answers prayers, not like we like sometimes, but He answers with what is best for us. I really believe Ted is your man. But, I won't push the issue. I just want you to be happy. Give it some time."

I did. Time passed. Ted never called. Thanksgiving rolled around and our young adults Sunday School class was having a pot-luck dinner at the church. Ted and I were the only two unmarried people in the class. Thrown together was a mild way of putting it. Everyone at church was pushing, I was resisting and, my dad was just watching.

The evening ended, with Ted asking to drive me home again. I said, "Okay," but I was dreading those fifteen minutes from the church to my house.

Pulling up in front, Ted stammered, "Wanna go to a movie Saturday? Momma said she likes you and I should get out more."

I thought about what my dad had said, and wondered if maybe he was right, about the prayers and God and faith. We had still been praying every night for the right man to come along. Maybe this was really it. Ted was really a good guy, he went to Church, and taught young boys in a mission group. Besides, why not? He's the only male in 500 miles asking me out. So, I muttered, "Okay, what time will you pick me up?"

Things moved along pretty well through December, Ted started coming to my house two and three times a week. My Dad was in his glory. My mother was on the phone with his mom more than usual. I was beginning to find more and more good points about Ted and his family.

Christmas came. I was hesitant to buy him a present because I didn't want him to think I was pushy or overly interested. Actually I was just passing the time with him until something better came along. Then two days before Christmas the florist delivered a beautiful batch of red and white carnations. The card was simply signed, "Ted".

Well, I had to get him something, now.

After Christmas, somehow the heat got turned up. Ted was at my house almost every evening. He was picking me up for church every Sunday and we were going to prayer meeting on Wednesday together. January passed and February snuck in. I knew what holiday was coming. I dreaded it. I couldn't figure out just what I was thinking. Thoughts about Ted were jumbled. Then on "The Day," I came home from work and there in the living room was a long white box.

"Oh, Mother how sweet, Daddy sent you flowers for Valentine's Day. That's really neat."

From the kitchen came, "Check again, the card says they're for you."

I looked and sure enough, the envelope had MY name on it. I opened the box to find a dozen long stemmed red roses. The card was signed, "Love, Ted".

"Love?" I thought. "Love?" My head was spinning. My heart was too surprised to beat normally. I just fell into the closest chair and said out loud, "Love?"

The next day was Saturday and there was a basketball tournament going on at the gym. Ted was one of the officials. Two of my girl friends and I decided to go. I had related the tale of the roses to them and they were really impressed. Becky asked, "How are you going to thank him?"

"Say, 'Thanks, Ted' I guess."

"Oh, come on, Anna, you can do better than that."

Barb knew me too well. We'd been friends for life, and she knew it was a fact that I would not turn down a dare.

"Dare you to kiss him in front of the team," she quipped.

"Oh...no."

"Oh...yeah."

"Okay, but only on the cheek."

We got to the gym, and lucky for me, Ted was coming down the steps as we were going up. I stopped him and thanked him for the roses and tip-toed to kiss his cheek.

"Sure," he stuttered. "Okay. Gotta go get lunch for the refs."

The roses, or my thanks triggered something in Ted. He started holding my hand or putting his arm around me in public. He even started kissing me goodnight.

I finally confided in my dad, "I think Ted really is the one. I love to be with him, I miss him when we're not together. Maybe...."

Needless to say, my dad was ecstatic.

We were married that July.

At a family reunion in August, one of my new sisters-in-law jokingly asked, "How did you get my little brother to say that "L" word and to finally commit?"

"He really did use "love" first, on the card with my Christmas roses. I was the first to kiss him, but...."

Before I could finish, Ted's Momma interrupted and sweetly said, "Anna, Ted didn't send those roses, I did. It was time that lug got himself a wife and left the nest. Twenty-seven is too old to be living at home with your Momma."

I guess our romantic helpers knew what they were doing, and they both had a private line to Heaven and had the Lord on their side. We've been married for thirty-two years!

FIRST STRING
by Danny Fulks

Janie Lee Wells stood in front of the bathroom vanity mirror. She watched her reflection in the smoked glass as she puffed up her white wool sweater with the letter B attached. Even the two-hour ritual of dressing in Barclay High's cheerleading uniform gave her a rush, thinking how that at seventeen being captain of the cheerleading squad and a potential valedictorian gave her an edge up. Within minutes she was behind the wheel of her daddy's new royal blue, freshly Simonized Buick Roadmaster headed toward Barclay High school. The sounds of the frenzied crowd inside the school gymnasium floated across the quadrangle and into the village of Jackson, Kentucky. It was Friday night and this was the last basketball game of regular season play for Barclay High school. Janie Lee was in her element.

As the end of the half-time break approached, the five starters and the second string players returned from the locker room, past the rows of fans who stood three deep along the walls of the matchbox-size gym. Barclay was ahead eight points and the anticipation of play in the county tournament gripped the Panthers and their followers. The fervor of Kentucky high school basketball was not a game. It was a religion. A town that had been nurtured over the years by Protestant, fundamental churches had succumbed to the sensual nature of the sport itself. Men and women whose ancestors had socialized at church revivals, pie suppers, and summer baptisms in Buckeye Creek had found a new form of salvation. The sanctuary was a gymnasium that smelled like sweat, cheap perfume, and tobacco. Instead of shouts of victory for Jesus and waving handkerchiefs, now there were yells for the Barclay Panthers. Thirteen high school boys dressed in lettered uniforms—five on the floor throughout the game, eight sitting on the bench, elbows on their knees hoping for a few minutes play in the last quarter after the score had been run up. Six cheerleaders, whose moves showed legs and tights that reflected in the buffed hardwood floor.

David Dale Gillette had authority wherever there was a basketball. Since he was ten years old and his uncle gave him one for Christmas, he had carried it with him wherever he went. In a world of relationships that spun around fate's impersonal ebbs, the basketball was always there for him. His father, Carlton, had died on the wrong end of a Saturday night special in the gravel parking lot of a roadhouse called the Blue Willow when David was three. And after his mother, Faith, took up with a drifter who had done time at Frankfort for grand theft, he was shipped off up George's Creek to live with his grandparents.

So it was there with Grandma and Grandpa Gillette, whom he called Mom and Pop, that David's beliefs were formed. These old people—Pop, who lived on three-hundred dollars a month that he drew down for black lung, and Mom, who spent her time frying chicken and reading the Bible— had done their best to raise David in the spirit of the Lord. Sometimes he felt like he was the only Christian boy around trying to whip loneliness with righteous living. The boys who hung out in the back room late into the night at Taylor's grocery store taught David a thing or two about five-card stud. Taught him so well that he became a fair poker player and with his cold, dark eyes, he even learned when to call, raise, pass, how much to bet to get a call, or bluff. But always on the floor beside him was the brown leather basketball, inflated daily to nine pounds. By the time he was fourteen, David was driving his grandpa's old 1941 Plymouth business coupe on roads close to home. He put fender skirts and blue-dotted tail lights on the old machine. Sharp. And with some of the other boys around the county that he loafed with, he began to do some thrill driving, like Joey Chitwood's Hell Drivers, sliding the rear of the car around curves on gravel roads, drag racing over on the main highway, driving with his arm around the young girls that were easy to pick up at the Frosty-Freeze.

The sound of the referee's whistle in the Barclay High School gym brought David Gillette, and four other team members to the middle of the floor for the jump ball. Six cheerleaders in black and white uniforms whirled and chanted from the floor, "David, David, he's our man/ If he can't do it, nobody can." An instant before he crouched for the long jump, David made eye contact with Janie Lee Wells. She, firm and in control, faced the home crowd and egged them on as attention focused on the behind-the-back passes of the Barclay forwards, Weston and Grimes. The Oswego Tigers, cross-county rivals in gold and green uniforms that sparkled in the reflection from the gym lights, played tough. Masters of the fast break and mean, they kept the Barclay fans on the defensive, and yells of "Shoot it, shoot, it," and "Elbow the jerks" added to the tension. But this ball game belonged to David

Gillette. The Barclay coach yelled, "Feed Gillette," and without hesitation the forwards guided the ball his way. A set-shot from thirty feet by Gillette got nothing but net. The Tigers returned with the next jump ball and on a fastbreak Weston scored on a layup. Near the end of the last quarter, however, two back-to-back hook shots by Gillette robbed the Tigers of any chance for victory. And when the time-clock jerked out the last second of play, the scoreboard read: HOME 42, VISITORS 39.

Across the lighted area of the parking lot where only a few cars were still parked, the running engine of the Buick made a pleasant sound and smell in the February night. Janie Lee sat behind the wheel. As she felt the warm air from the heater, in her mind she was with her first love, Jim Jack White, at his parent's house at Christmastime. She saw him as his long fingers opened his Christmas present. She saw herself at the dinner table with his family. It was dark and the daylight was short but the fire burned warm and the cherry pie tasted good. And again he and she sat in a back pew at a revival service in a country church while the choir sang in low sweet harmony:

"O, why not tonight?
O, why not tonight?
Wilt thou be saved?
Then why not tonight."

She saw Jim Jack driving through the village past her family's house in his father's pick-up truck and he waved to her in the summer heat. She saw them together on another summer night in her bedroom and they were alone in the house. She saw the white plastic radio that sat on her night stand and the lighted dial projected large in her mind and diminished the scary way their breaths were joined.

She grinned and was relieved when she saw David as he walked to the car, opened the passenger door, and eased into the soft, warm passenger seat.

"Get in, Dave, it's late," Janie Lee said.

"How did I look out there tonight?"

"I don't know," Janie answered, "I thought McKenzie played a great game."

"Sure, sure, what did he get, three minutes off the bench?"

"Just kidding. You were sharp. You're always sharp."

As they moved on down the night road, David's eyes swept across the car's dashboard highlighted in the darkness by its lighted radio dial, large round speedometer, and white plastic knobs. Janie Lee gunned the car forward, down a long straight stretch—fifty-sixty-seventy-eighty—the speedometer read as they sped off. The bleak hillsides and the black, bare trees seemed to flash past the car windows like a movie run at fast speed. The sparse flats in the hills were without signs of life. And on the west side of the road, on the narrow strips of bottom land, frozen corn stalks glistened.

"There's a pint under the seat," Janie said.

"Yeah, I got it."

The pint of Seagram's Crown Royal that Janie had sneaked out of her parents' house was small in David's hands. He twisted the cap, pressed the top of the bottle against his upper lip, worked two or three sips into his mouth, and handed it to Janie. She took a drink, grimaced, and gave David one of those, "Ain't we a bunch of knuckleheads," looks. David pulled a pack of Lucky Strike cigarettes from his shirt pocket, shook two out, lit them both from the car's lighter and passed one over to Janie. David sucked the smoke down into his lungs, exhaled, and took another deep drag. Janie, after two or three short puffs from her cigarette, crushed it into the ash tray and chanted, "L-S-M-F-T, Lucky Strike Means Fine Tobacco." Hank Williams' voice came in clear through the car's radio speakers: "There was a time when I believed that you belonged to me/ But now I know my heart is shackled to a memory...." And as the whiskey began to seep into his head, David could see Janie Lee Wells walking up the broad stairway at Barclay High, in yellow pedal pushers on a warm spring day. He saw them alone in a skiff on the lake in deep summer and heard her giggle as she poked her bare foot gently into his ribs. In his mind, he was with Janie Lee in his grandpa's 1941 Plymouth, and it was early autumn, and he could feel the warmth of her body as they hugged inside the parked car.

"Slide over here," Janie said.

The speedometer read eighty-five now as the road again straightened out, the fence posts along the highway flew past, and the heavy Roadmaster with its four chrome port holes on each fender purred, gliding over the long, low dips in the road.

"You know what, Janie," David said.

"No, what?"

"You're one scary woman."

"How come?"

"I don't know. It's just the way you are. You get your dad's car, you steal his whiskey, you drive like a fool, like a boy, really. We could wind up dead, you know. Get our names on the front page of that paper your dad puts out."

"Don' sweat it, OK."

Parked now by the church graveyard, David moved over to the passenger side of the car, let another sip of whiskey slide down his throat, pulled the car's cigarette lighter out and pressed it to the tip of another Lucky. Janie Lee slid across the seat toward him, turned around, placed her knees on the seat, and leaned back against the car's dashboard, her hands resting on David's shoulders.

"Janie," David said, "I think you know, even though I'm not much of a talker. I mean...can't you tell...you can tell, you're not dumb."

"You've been good to me. Real good when I needed you a lot. The first time I made it as a cheerleader some of the girls said my daddy had got it for me. That I wouldn't have got it on my own. And we talked that day after school for a long time. You never believed any of that."

"No, I figured you earned it. Who's sharper than you? I've never saw any other girl I really cared about. But in three months we're going out of here. You'll probably go off to school. I've got a scholarship with Rupp at U.K. if I want it. But who wants to lay around some place four years without money?"

"David, you're a sweet guy."

David pulled Janie Lee in close. She came forward easy into his arms and pressed her face against his cheek and whispered, "Love me, David." David Dale Gillette just squeezed his eyes shut tight, let his muscles go limp, and pulled out yet another smoke. He untangled his body from Janie, opened the car door, got out and lit up. He stood for awhile leaning against the car, smoking, feeling the cold, damp air that hung close to the ground. Janie's suggestion and the night cold sharpened his brain. He flipped the cigarette butt off toward the graveyard, walked around the car and got in the driver's side. He wished to God she had never said that, just kept her mouth shut.

"Come on, Janie baby, I'll drive this doosey back to Jackson." Not saying anything he drove with Janie Lee cuddled up next to him. Thirty minutes later they were back at the high school parking lot.

"Maybe it'll go better next time." Janie said.

"Yeah, I guess maybe. See you Monday."

"Right." David waved as he walked in front of the Buick toward the old Plymouth. At home a coal fire banked with ashes cast a warm, orange glow and created weird shadows on the walls and furniture. David knew his grandmother was awake and lying in bed with his grandfather in their bedroom. He was quiet, though, and after smoking one last cigarette, slipped off into his cold bedroom, hung his clothes on nails in the wall, and snuggled under the homemade comforts.

Friday night's sounds and smells clung to David through the weekend. But when Monday morning came he walked into Barclay High school with authority and grace.

"Hey, David," yelled Jack Weston.

"What?" said David.

"Did you hear about Janie Lee Wells? Did you know what she did over the weekend?"

"What's that?"

"She got married. Run off with Jim Jack White."

"Come on, are you crazy?"

"I ain't kidding you, David, she did. They took off Saturday morning, drove down to Johnson City, Tennessee, and got married. I heard them talking down at the office."

"What makes you think I care? You tell everybody, will you? Just tell them I don't care what Janie Lee Wells did."

David walked off alone to the boys' restroom, and as the school bell rang and quiet came over the building, sat in silence in one of the stalls. Thinking now he had to get the hell out of there, he ran outside the building and jumped into the Plymouth. He grabbed the plastic spinner on the car's steering wheel with his left hand, started the engine, revved it up and took off between the school buses still parked on the lot. Gravel from the car's spinning wheels pelted the area as he dropped the clutch. Students stared in awe.

When David was clear of the village on the road out of town, he pressed the car's gas pedal to the floor and took the car to its top speed, maybe eighty-five. As he moved into a right turn grasping the steering wheel spinner, he dropped the right front wheel off the blacktop onto the grassy shoulder, broke adhesion from the blacktop with the rear wheels, held the gas pedal down hard and steered left. Through the curve, he pulled the spinner back to the right as the car's rear end whipped back onto the road. White lines, yellow lines, guard rails, fence posts, and cattle in the fields all flipped by like cheap pictures from a Big Little Book. David wondered what everyone would think if he rolled the car over the bank and flipped it two or three times into the shallow creek that ran near the highway. They'd probably let school out for that. Hell, it wouldn't take that much nerve. He pulled the car to the left side of the road, dropped both wheels off the shoulder, and kept the pedal down. One flip left on the spinner and it would be twisted metal, broken glass and weeds wedged behind chrome. But still there was roundball and the county tournament. Maybe even the state. Or playing for Rupp at U.K. All those beers to drink, the cigarettes left to smoke. He eased his foot off the gas, pulled back to the right side of the road, slowed the car and pulled off into the parking area of Taylor's Grocery and Gas Station.

"Ain't you supposed to be in school, young Gillette?" came the man's voice behind the counter inside the store.

"Maybe yes, maybe no. Give me a pack of Luckies." Lighting up, he listened to the voice that came from the radio behind the counter "…the United Nations Forces checked a Communist drive at Amidong in Eastern Korea and were within thirty miles of the Thirty-eighth Parallel. With the intensity of the 'police action' and the heavy commitment of the United States to the United Nations forces, it appears that efforts to draft young Americans will be stepped up."

David thought about something his buddy, Jack Weston, had said to him not too long ago, "Dave, I'll join up if you will. Maybe hit the Air Force or the Navy. Beat the Army and Truman's draft."

LAURA
by Loyal Jones

John Williams' heart quickened when he topped the hill and saw the school. He drew the mare down to a walk. She pranced sideways, but he held her with heel and bit.

"You're feeling your oats today," he observed and lifted her to a gentle canter. Dismounting and hitching the mare to a sapling, he patted her on the shoulder as he turned to go up the steps. Pushing open the heavy door, he was startled as always by the bell that rang harshly above his head. A door across the hall opened, and a woman emerged to stare sharply.

"Can I help you, John?"

"Well, yes, Miss Larkin, I'm here to see Laura."

"Was she expecting you?" Her tone was as pointed as her stare.

"I told her I'd come today."

"I thought she was working on her grades," she said, reproach in her voice, but she went to the stairs and called Laura's name and reentered her room with a final look.

He saw her neat ankles first, as she skimmed down the stairs. She wore a white blouse with her dark hair spilling over it, and her eyes, brown as chestnuts and dark-lashed, made his breath catch.

"I'm glad you came," she said and drew close. He cradled her elbows in his hands and kissed her. She trembled but withdrew.

"Let's walk," she said, and they went out to where the mare stood nervously pawing the ground.

"How're you, Lucy?" she asked, putting her hand out as the mare moved forward and bumped her head against the girl's shoulder.

"She's fine," he said, "but frisky. I haven't worked her today, but she's about ready for the fair, I reckon."

They walked the path into the woods, and when they were out of sight of the school, he took her hand and squeezed it, feeling inadequate in what he wanted to say. She squeezed back, and they went on. At last he stopped, taking her in his arms, "I love you more than anything in the world." He kissed her and held her close, then leaned back, looking down at her lowered eyes and the bright tear on her cheek.

"I love you too. You know that," she said, but misery clouded her features.

"Then, why don't we just get married?"

"It's not that easy," her dark eyes reddened. You know I'm engaged to Philip, and my parents are determined for me to marry him."

"But do you love him?" He hungered for the answer he sought.

"Yes, at least I thought I did until I met you. Philip and I have known each other all our lives, and our families are close. I can't face disappointing them."

"What about disappointing me and yourself?"

"I know." After a while she said, "Look, my parents are coming to take me home this week-end, and I want them to meet you. Let's not talk about it until after you meet them. O.K.?"

"It ought to be just between you and me. Yet, I can see the bind you're in, but I want you to know that my whole world changed when you came here to teach. I can't stand to think of losing you."

She kissed him, "I love you, too. Let's go back. I have to finish my grades."

She held his hand on the walk back, which kept him from arguing further. She wiped her eyes and tried to smile, but her pale face was glum. She kissed him again briefly at the door, "Come for lunch Saturday to meet my parents."

He mounted the anxious Lucy and racked her home. After she drank from the trough, he put her in a stall and fed her and the other whickering horses. His cattle dog Buster came to him, with ears back and wagging tail, and John sent him for Rosie, the milk cow. When he returned from the house with the milk bucket, Buster had Rosie, at the gate. He fed her, milked her, and turned her back into the pasture and poured milk for the barn cats. He found his mother in the kitchen, bending over the stove. He kissed her on the top of her head as he went to the sink to wash his hands and strain the milk. He was silent for most of the meal, and his mother watched him narrowly.

"Were you working Lucy?" she asked.

"Not really. I rode her over to the school to see Laura." He didn't look up as he talked, and his mother studied him.

"How are you two doing? Do you love her?"

He chewed for a time, looking up with a trace of a smile, "Yeah, I guess you could say that. I've asked her to marry me, but as I told you, she's promised to a guy back home, and I'm afraid his prospects are better than mine. Her parents will be here Saturday, and she wants us to meet."

"That may mean something," his mother said. "I don't know

much to say about this, but I tell you one thing, you don't have to be ashamed of who you are. You're as good as any of her city people. Your father was an honest and good man, and so are you. We're not rich, but we are decent folks. You know that, don't you?"

He nodded, "Yes, and as you've told me, money isn't everything." He paused. "I just don't know her world, or her people. I don't know what she will do when she goes back home this summer."

His mother looked at him sorrowfully and said, "I do wish you could have finished college before your father died."

"Yeah," he said, "but a college degree wouldn't help us here on the farm, and I don't think it would impress her folks, either."

He helped her with the dishes, and they read awhile before saying good night.

Early on Saturday morning, he worked the three horses that he boarded and trained. The three-year-old, bucked and shied, and he had to keep his mind on staying aboard. The other two were seasoned performers, and he put them through their gaits briskly. Then he saddled Lucy and worked her with satisfaction until her coat darkened with sweat.

"You'll beat them all again this year," he said affectionately, as he sponged her and rubbed her dry. He turned her out in a small pasture to graze, and looked at his watch.

He went to the house, showered and put on khakis and his best sport coat. He considered a tie but hung it back on the rack, combed his hair and went to find his mother. She was working in her flower garden.

"Do you think I'll pass inspection?"

She rose and looked him over fondly. "You pass mine. If they've got the sense of a goose, you'll pass theirs too. I think Laura's already passed on you, if that's all there was to it."

"We'll see, won't we." He kissed her on the cheek and went out to his pickup and drove slowly, dreading the encounter. A black Lincoln with Missouri plates loomed in the parking lot, and he parked beside it. He checked his image in the mirror before going in.

Laura sat on the bench with her parents in the hallway, and they turned toward him at the noise of the bell. She rose but did not come forward. He saw that her good looks came from her mother, who also had dark eyes and hair that now was sprinkled with grey. Her father, in coat and tie, was tall and spare, with a trimmed mustache and close-clipped grey hair. "Bankers have to keep up appearances," he thought.

"This is my father and mother," she said, her voice unnatural. "And this is John Williams. He's been very kind to me this year. He's taken me horseback riding several times. He has wonderful horses."

John advanced to shake hands with her father, who shook firmly and smiled cordially but observed him closely. Mrs. Demetrius extended her hand with a reserved smile, but he thought her eyes did not smile.

"I understand that you train horses," Mr. Demetrius said.

"Yes, I do, among other things. Mainly, I run a farm, raise corn, hay, some cattle, keep four broodmares and take a few horses for training."

"What kind of horses?"

"Saddlebreds. They're show and pleasure horses, all five-gaited. My father raised them, and I grew up riding them. We show them at county fairs and other shows. Everybody's got to have some kind of passion, I guess."

"I'd like to see them perform," Mrs. Demetrius broke in.

"I'll be happy to show them to you," he said.

Laura looked more at ease. "I think lunch is ready," she

said and led them to the dining room, where Miss Larkin and another teacher were seated by a window. They waved.

"It must be pretty hard farming here in these mountains," Mr. Demetrius said, after they had served themselves.

He detected that this was not a casual question. "Yes, it's not the best place in the country, but my family has farmed here for three generations and made a living at it." He added, "Up to now anyway. It's getting harder for the little farmer to make a go of it. Cattle prices are down, but I notice that doesn't affect the price of meat in the supermarket. I guess the big companies know how to protect their profits. The little farmer can't."

Demetrius studied him with narrowed eyes and observed, "Profit is the name of the game, and the bigger you are the more control you have. Consolidation is the key to the future. My bank was just bought out by a national bank."

"Well," he said, "I can't buy out other farms, and I don't intend to sell ours. So I guess that leaves me between a rock and a hard place."

"Do you make money with your horses?" her father continued.

"Yes, sometimes, when we have a good foal and get it trained right and find a good buyer. But, it costs quite a bit to go to the fairs, and the prize money is not that much. I do pretty well with the boarding and training, but I keep only three or four at a time. I guess I don't do it for the money, when you get down to it."

"Really," said Mrs. Demetrius, eyebrows arched.

"You have to think of the bottom line." Demetrius said. "Have the elimination of farm subsidies hurt you."

"Yeah, some, but we never got much anyway. A lot of

little farmers will go out of business though. Most of the subsidy money went to the big farms."

"Mr. Demetrius spoke sharply: "I never heard that, but we have to get rid of these give-away programs and balance the budget."

"Except for the big corporations that get their welfare," John said, his voice clearly betraying his irritation. "You can rest assured that the budget will be balanced on the backs of poor people, farmers, workers—those that don't have political clout."

"What do you mean, welfare?" Mr. Demetrius' mustache quivered a bit. Laura was troubled at the direction of the conversation.

"I mean, practically every congressman and senator has pushed through some sort of special subsidy, tax-break, or outright grant to his favorite back-home company, especially if it contributes generously to his campaign fund."

"But that's so they can establish overseas markets and create new jobs, I'm sure," Laura said, hoping to fend off an argument. She could see that her father was getting upset and she desperately aimed a warning look at John."

But John couldn't stop.

"Look who's laying people off and moving to countries where they can get cheaper labor. It's the very corporations getting federal grants, that's who."

'I just don't know where you're getting those ideas," Mr. Demetrius said, his voice rising. "Times are changing, and we have to change with them. It's a global economy and corporations move overseas so they can make things cheaper. That's what business is all about."

"That's why I have a dim view of business."

"O.K., O.K., let's talk about something else," Laura broke

in, her eyes flashing. "I want to tell you about my students. You know, most of them board here during the year, and many come from poor or broken homes, but they do so well."

"Maybe that's because you are a good teacher," John added, and her parents nodded with pride, although Mr. Demetrius, still flushed, avoided looking at him.

"Well, I do the best I can with them," she said, "but they are bright and willing. I'm so proud of them. I'll miss them."

"You mean during the summer?" John asked.

"Well, yes," she said, but she didn't look at him. Her parents exchanged glances, and he noticed that something went unsaid between them.

"Could we go see your horses?" Mrs. Demetrius asked after dessert.

"Of course," he said.

"I'll ride with John, and you can follow," Laura said. Her mother looked as if she would like to question this arrangement, but she nodded. He held the door for Laura, and then got in, started the truck, backed out, and drove slowly the two miles to his farm.

"You sure pushed a few buttons," she said.

"Well you know by now how I feel about politics and corporations," he said, "and I guess your folks need to know how I feel." He stopped in front of his house.

He walked around the car to speak to her parents, "Come in. I want you to meet my mother."

They walked up the path to the front porch, where John's mother was waiting. After introductions, she went inside for iced tea. They drank tea and looked across the valley toward the mountains.

"This is a beautiful place you have here, Mrs. Williams." Mrs. Demetrius said, and her husband nodded enthusiastically.

"Yes, I never grow tired of this view," his mother said. "My husband came out here to watch every pretty sunset."

"How long has he been gone?" Mrs. Demetrius asked.

"Four years, this July," she said, and the Demetriuses nodded sympathetically.

In the pasture, Lucy threw up her head and nickered. She trotted toward the barn, her coat glinting in the sun.

"I'll show you the horses," John said. They all walked to the barn and went inside. Lucy whinnied loudly at being ignored while he showed them the three boarding horses and then pointed through the hallway to the brood mares with their young foals grazing with the cattle beyond the barn. He took a bridle from the tack room and walked to the gate where the mare waited. Leading her inside, he saddled her, mounted, and rode to the training ring, starting off at a brisk trot. Reining her in, he set her into her rocking chair canter for a turn. Then he slow-gaited her for a round and a half and let her go at a full rack, her head and tail high and her legs moving with exaggerated action. Streaks of sweat darkened the mare's bright skin, so he slowed her and rode out of the ring.

"She is a beautiful animal," Mr. Demetrius said. I don't know much about Saddlebreds, but I'm impressed by her disposition and her great movement."

"Yeah, she's a wonderful mare," he said. "I love Saddlebreds."

Mrs. Demetrius moved up to rub the mare's fine head, "She is just gorgeous," she said, then "George, we'd better be going. Lucy wants to show us her classroom, and she wants us to see some of the countryside."

Laura hung back as they walked toward the car. "Come over tonight about nine. My parents will have gone back to the motel by then, and we can talk. I'm afraid that Daddy wants to leave early tomorrow morning."

"All, right," he said, and tried to hide his disappointment that she was really leaving so soon. "I'll see you then."

He fed and watered the horses, sent Millie off to round up Rosie, then went for the milk bucket and fed the cow. He feared that if Laura left she would never return.

"I'm going over to see Laura later on after her folks go back to the motel." He said over supper. "They're leaving in the morning."

"Do you think she'll come back?"

"I don't know. She says she wants to come back and teach next fall, but I'm afraid that she never will. I'm sure that her parents want to get her away from here, and from me."

"I don't know what to say. Maybe she needs the summer to decide what it is she wants. If, in the end, she doesn't come back, maybe that's best for you, even if it seems like more than you can stand now."

"I know you're right," he said and carried the dishes to the sink. He washed them while she sat at the table and they discussed farming matters to avoid further talk about Laura.

They sat in the living room and both took up books, although he could not keep his mind on Wendell Berry's story about an old farmer who reminded him of his father. Finally it was time to go, and he kissed his mother and said good night.

He drove up to the front of the school and waited until Laura emerged, slipping into the pickup beside him, "Let's take a ride." She sat close as he turned around, drove to the main road, and headed toward town.

"My parents enjoyed meeting you and your mother--also seeing the horses," she said.

"I doubt that they enjoyed meeting me," he said.

128 • *Appalachian Love Stories*

She spoke softly, "John, you have to understand that they see you as a threat. They want me back in St. Louis. I love you because you're so different from anyone I ever knew back there, but they see your difference too, and they're afraid. They resent anyone who's different from them. They just want what's best for me."

"What have you told them about us?"

"That I love you, that I have been happy here this year, but that I still care for Philip and that I am going to have to make up my mind what I want to do. I'm sure they think that when I get back to St. Louis, I'll be content there."

"Are they right?"

"I don't think so, but I don't know. I need some time to think. Can you understand that?"

"No, not really, to be honest with you. I know that you're torn, but I love you so much and I believe you love me too."

"Oh, John, I know, and I do love you" she said and brought his hand to her lips.

He pulled into the Sonic drive-in at the edge of town. They ordered milkshakes and waited miserably until they came. He turned on the radio to Merle Haggard singing, "What am I gonna do with the rest of my life?"

He sighed, "That's a good question, if you don't come back."

She leaned her head against his shoulder and groaned. He put the truck in gear, backed out and headed back. Haggard finished and Tom T. Hall sang about "Old dogs and children, and watermelon wine." She sat with her head against his shoulder. Sammi Smith sang, "Help Me Make It Through The Night." He turned off the radio and was silent until he parked out of sight of the school.

He took her in his arms and kissed her forlornly, and she kissed him back. He turned the radio on again, and they lay in each other's arms without talking. He dozed, and when he awoke, the announcer gave the time as past midnight. She stirred, and said, "I've got to go."

"You will call and write?" he asked.

"Yes, but can you give me some time?"

"All right," he said, his heart heavy. She kissed him once more, swung out of the truck and ran to the door. In the dimness he saw her dark hair and her pale face. She waved and disappeared.

He drove home slowly, parked, and went in quietly. His mother had left a light on for him. He undressed quickly and got in bed. He lay awake a long time before sleeping.

He rose early the next morning to do the milking and to feed the horses. His mother looked at him inquiringly when he returned but busied herself with making breakfast. They ate silently for a few moments, and then he said, "Well, she's gone, and she wants me to give her time to make up her mind."

She nodded, "I'm sorry. It's not going to be easy for you to wait."

"I'll give her as much time as she wants. I've had my say and it's up to her."

His mother reached across the table and clasped his arm. "I hope she realizes what a treasure you are," she said.

"Well, you're prejudiced." He paused as if to add something but got his cap and went out and down to the barn. He worked the other horses, then Lucy, her faultless gaits so pleasing to him that he forgot Laura for a while. Lucy's muscled body rippled beneath him, and her high arched neck and slender ears were almost level with his eyes. Her canter was so collected and rhythmic that he hugged her neck impulsively. When he put her into a slow gait, her head came up even higher, her singlefooting action reminding him of the working of a fine watch. When he let her rack on, he sat as easily as if she ran on wheels. He was happy as he rubbed her down and turned her into the side pasture to graze.

The days passed slowly, so he kept himself busy with the horses and the countless tasks of a working farm. He planted corn and a field of soybeans. He cut and baled the first growth of hay. When the corn was ready for its first cultivation, he still had not heard from Laura. Still, he did not write or call. He ate less and he slept poorly. He grew leaner, and his mother watched and worried.

After six weeks had passed, he woke one morning and knew that he had waited long enough. After breakfast, he returned to his room and took down pen and paper and wrote:

Dear Laura,

I love you as I will no other, but I know by now that your mind is either made up, or too unsettled for me to hope longer. These weeks have been harder than any I have ever spent. My heart breaks each day when I wake to think of you. I cannot live this way, so I write to say goodbye and to wish you well in the decision that you have made, or to make it easier for you to make a decision. I have to get on with my life, even if it is to be one of dreadful loneliness, and I pray that time will lessen that. I love you

John

He mailed the letter and then told his mother of his decision. She hugged him and told him she had feared it would turn out this way.

Lucy won the blue ribbon at the county fair and two other shows. He prepared the other horses for their owners to ride in several shows. He looked ahead.

He never heard from Laura again.

THE FIDDLE AND THE FRUIT JAR
by Billy C. Clark

Pa's fiddle hung in its case from a rusted nail on the wall of the bedroom. This had been its resting place since the day he and Ma had first gone to housekeeping in the valley of the Big Sandy. And through the years it had remained the only competition that my mother ever had. I say competition because it was often declared here by the hill folk that a fiddle player had a wanderer's foot. You could not change the ways of a fiddle player. Ma knew this. And so, a young bride, she allowed the fiddle to become a part of their marriage. In all of Pa's travels over the valley the sweet music of his fiddle would be loved the most at home. Ma presented him with eight children, more than a good set for a square dance, and in all years of our growing up I'm sure that the fiddle never caused her a jealous moment.

After Pa came home from work at his small cobbler's shop we used to gather in the center of the floor and wait for the music of his lonesome fiddle. We learned early that there was a story in each of his ballads. We couldn't afford books, but we learned to read each pull of his bow as if it were a printed page.

Each night ended the same way, with the eight of us quarreling for Pa to play a different ballad. And always Ma would scold and threaten to have Pa put the fiddle back in the battered case. Afraid he might, we quieted as Pa pat-patted his foot and struck up an old familiar song…Ma's favorite. He was sure to play this song as soon as a frown touched Ma's face, grinning and bringing a smile back to her face.

The song was a ballad of love, so bold that it made my older brothers and sisters blush. I was too young to understand love. I liked to hear Pa play it simply because it brought such smiles to Ma's face, and gave me courage to argue again for my favorite song.

By the time I was old enough to really know my father, he had fiddled his hair white to match the white pine resin dust that his bow had left under the strings. The fiddle had traveled with him over every foot of the Big Sandy country: to square dances where feet flew into the air like brown leaves in an autumn wind; to funerals where his fiddle hummed of death; to holy baptizing in the waters of the Big Sandy River. There had been ballads for all occasions. Pa had gained the reputation of being the greatest of the "old-time fiddlers" among the hills of Kentucky.

But now white-haired, Pa was farther away from his fiddle than he had ever been. Only his dreams could touch it as it hung inside the battered case on the wall. He was bedfast from a stroke, the third within a year. He lay quarreling over the doctor bills coming, saying Ma needed the meager amount of money to buy food for the table.

The doctor had not given much promise. Either of the first two strokes had been great enough to have killed Pa. But he had proved by two recoveries that he was as stubborn and tough as the hills around him. This was the best encouragement the doctor could give.

But Ma had caught something in Pa's eyes that the doctor could not see. It was not the paralyzing of his body she saw there, but the paralyzing of his mind and spirit.

In the days that followed, Ma rested her eyes often on the battered fiddle case. She attributed untold powers to it, believing that if she could coax Pa to find courage to take it from the wall, the pull of the bow over the strings would strengthen and mend his body. But Ma had less time now for coaxing. She left the house early to find housework. She scrubbed floors on her hands and knees, and stretched her little body to wash down walls. Of the evenings, she brought home baskets of clothes and washed them with her hands into the late night. These hours of labor brought us food. And she sat on the edge of Pa's bed and fed him as she would have a small child, knowing that each bite he took reminded him of his helplessness and paralyzed him a little more.

It was not easy for Pa to remain flat on his back. He had worked hard all his life. He had begun in the small belly mines of the mountain country, then found his craft as a shoe cobbler. He had learned to work miracles with his hands. Weaving the needle in and out of leather that he had softened by hand, he built shoes for clubfooted children and covered scars and afflictions that couldn't be shod by machine-made shoes.

It shamed me to see an old man such as Pa have tears in his eyes as Ma fed him. Never once did it occur to me that he might have been looking at my mother's red hands, cracked until they bled over the rough washboard. Or that he might have been thinking it was a man's place to bring food to the table. I knew only that he had told me over the years that I should feel ashamed for crying. A man never cried.

One evening Ma came home from work and found the fiddle gone. She trembled as she spoke to Pa. "Where is the fiddle?"

Pa fought to raise his hand and Ma reached to take it in hers. And when they met, Pa slipped something to her. She unfolded the wrinkled dollar bills and they fell to the floor.

"You...you had no right to do it," she sobbed. "I'm no better to provide than you've been doing all these years." And she could not say more.

Pa never was much of a talker. "A talking man never hears," he had always taught us kids. And without practice himself, he failed miserably on this night. He could not convince Ma that he would remain paralyzed forever. She cried softly, believing that the only medicine to cure him was now gathering dust in the corner of the secondhand store—sold for little more than she could have earned with a few washings. Yet this pitiful sum had made Pa believe he had lightened Ma's burden. His eyes, wandering to rest on the rusted nail, sadly told us that what he had done had not been easy.

Often of the evenings, I would go to meet Ma and help her carry the washings home. I was the smallest of four boys and the only one too young to be ashamed of being seen carrying them, telling all within sight that we were as poor as the red clay hills around us.

Each day Ma stopped at the secondhand store, leaving me outside guarding the clothes. This was one of Ma's queer new ways I could not understand. For instance, a few days earlier I had seen her stuffing something inside an empty fruit jar in the basement and then hiding the jar. After she had gone I sneaked the jar into the open and saw money in it. I just could not understand why she would be hiding money from us when there was so little to eat.

I sneaked each evening to see the jar until she finally caught me. She said, "What little money there is inside the jar wouldn't fill your tooth. It's the love tucked around it that fills the jar."

It just didn't make sense. I didn't know that old people had love. I thought it belonged only to the young, like my brother who was sparking a girl who lived nearby.

I went with Ma the morning she took the money from the jar. After we had picked up a heaping basket of clothes to be washed, we stopped at the secondhand store. I stood guarding the basket and she went inside. When she came out she had the battered fiddle case under her arm. She tucked it under the clothes, and warned me not to speak of it when we reached home.

That night Pa quarreled at Ma for spending her hard-earned money to bring the fiddle back to just gather dust on the wall. But his tired old eyes had changed and they lied on him this time. There was tenderness inside them that we all recognized as we peeked around the door.

Ma scolded us back to bed and we cocked our ears hoping to hear the fiddle again. But no sound of music came. Since I was the smallest and the lightest on foot I was chosen to sneak again to the door and tell what I saw.

Here is what I told them: I saw my father lift his arm by his own strength and brush tears from my mother's eyes.

He tried to play the fiddle. He tried to play Ma's favorite...the one he always used to put her in a happy mood...the song he had first played many years ago when he had come to court her. And although we heard nothing but the squeak of the bow held by a crippled hand, I think that to them it was the softest, sweetest ballad he had ever played.

Melungeon Marriage*
by Jesse Stuart

With a table, bed, stove, two chairs, with bedding and quilts Deutsia had made, dishes and kitchen utensils she had gathered and the ones I had brought from the shanty, our house was furnished. We sat before our own fireplace, where the bright crackling flames threw out enough heat to warm us and to light our room.

"This is the prettiest place on this mountain, Dave," Deutsia said as she looked over the room where light and shadow played on the smooth walls. "I'm proud of our home."

"It's better than a rock cliff. Maybe this house will inspire our people to make better ones."

"Sure it will," she said. "They'll be trying to build one like ours. You wait and see. They'll ask you why you built a place like this."

"I'll tell 'em I had to have a pretty cage for a pretty bird."

"Oh, it's heaven to be in our home!"

"Your folks were kind to us," I said. "I never stayed at a place in my life where I was treated nicer and had food that I liked better."

"I like to hear you say that, Dave," Deutsia said, her face beaming with joy. "I'm glad to hear a kind word spoken for my people, but there's not any place in the world like your own home."

"It's well anchored against the wind here," I said. "The big chimney will help hold us, and the logs are well notched. If the wind turns us over, our house won't come apart."

"Then you're afraid of the storms up here, Dave?"

"I am after seeing that one the night we found the cliff," I said. "I'll never forget that night."

"Neither will I," Deutsia said. "That was the first night we spent together." My chair was close to Deutsia's and our arms were around each other as we watched the bright tongues of flame leap from the dry cedar logs, rich resined pine knots and dry-seasoned yellow-locust sticks.

"Now I'm going to put one bed you make for us right over in that corner," Deutsia said. "I'm going to put a table stand over by the window. I'm going to put the cedar chest over on this side. I know where I'm going to put everything you make. When are you going to start making our furniture?"

"Tomorrow."

"What are you going to make first?"

"Some good chairs. And when I get the chairs made, what do you want me to make next?"

"The cedar chest, so we can put things in it."

"And then?"

"A walnut bed."

"I've already got the trees spotted," I said. "They are dead trees already seasoned."

"I've always wanted a pretty home," Deutsia said. "And when spring comes I'll show you how to make it prettier here. You just wait until I gather my wild flowers and bring them in here and put them in this yard and you'll see."

"I want to help you."

"Dave, there is something I want to tell you," Deutsia said, turning her eyes from the flaming fire. "I'm going to give you a present next spring.... I mean it, Dave," she said, before I could start my question.

"Why didn't you tell me before?"

"I wasn't sure," she said. "But I'm sure now."

"Oh, that's the best news." Before the fire, in our own little smoothwalled room, I pulled her carefully over to me, her beautiful face beneath mine, her golden hair streaming down to the floor, and I bent over until my lips met her lips. I held her there and kissed her while the light of the dancing flames flickered over her hair and the dry wood crackled.

"We moved just in time," I said. "Look out the window."

"That looks like a deep snow," Deutsia said. She raised her head from the pillow, looked out the window at a mountain world changed from dark and brown to white. "It's a pretty world. I like the changes of the seasons here, white, green, brown, and"—her voice trembled—"dark, all are pretty."

"This won't bother me from my work," I said. "I've got my wood here to make the chairs. I've got my tools here. I can work inside."

"That will be better. You'll be closer to me."

"And we've got dry wood to burn."

"If the snow stays on very long and we get short of supplies," Deutsia said, "we can get them from Bass and Daid. They always store and can for the winter, in spring, summer and autumn. They know what winter means up here."

"If we were to run out of supplies and couldn't get them up here," I said, "we'd never be able to get off the mountain now."

"Not when there's this much snow on the ground," she said. "It always drifts down by the second cliffs. I've seen drifts twenty feet deep there."

"Why do we mind the weather?" I asked Deutsia. "We've built walls and a roof against it. Why should we even talk about the weather? We're snug in our little place. We can even sleep as late as we want to on a morning like this." Then Deutsia lay her head on my arm, pulled up close to me, and I pulled the quilts upon us. Though a gray morning light had come to the white mountain world, we would not rise at an early hour on that morning.

Before the great snow had melted and gorged the mountain streams, I had finished our chairs. I had made two rockers and six straight-backed chairs. While I worked, Deutsia would cook meals for us and we'd eat at our little table together. After we'd eaten, I'd go back to my whittling, planing, and sandpapering, and putting arms and legs together. As soon as Deutsia was through with the dishes, she would help me. She would hold the pieces together with wooden pins or bore holes to fit rungs into the legs.

When the snow had melted, leaving drifts here and there, I went with my ax to the dead, seasoned black walnuts and wild cherries that I had found on the mountains. I chopped these trees down, trimmed their branches and topped them. And then I chopped two straight dead cedars that would split easily. I got Bass' mule and dragged these logs to the house so I would have plenty to do when another snow fell.

*This story is an excerpt from Stuart's novel, *Daughter of The Legend*.

BRANCH DANCE
by Linda Scott DeRosier

In the first dew of evening, Brenda Staniford plopped into the old wicker rocker on Grandma Banks's porch to savor her respite from the city. She raised her iced tea glass in mock salute to the cross-the-road neighbor, Tilton Butcher, who sat on his top step finishing his last cup of coffee of the day. As she sipped the sweet tea, Brenda noticed her friend Sudie scoot around their screen door and ease down into the porch swing to join Tilt in resting at the end of the long summer's day. From her grandmother's porch Brenda had watched this pattern every evening since she had come to visit. Sometimes Tilt and Sudie didn't exchange a word, though now and then one would make a remark that did not seem to require an answer. Much of the time they just kept a companionable silence as they listened to the frog and cricket chorus ushering in evening's twilight.

They had been sharing each other's space for the more than twenty-five years since they'd "had to" get married before Sudie turned fifteen, so Tilt and Sudie tended not to have much direct conversation. Like a lot of couples, they had lived into a place where they spent time together, each keeping his or her own counsel. In the past Sudie had been perpetually busy tending the couple's four children, while Tilt farmed, did a little pick up carpentry, and took care of the homeplace. Now, with their youngest married off two years ago, Sudie and Tilt had more opportunity to talk, but not much to say to each other.

On this particular summer evening, however, Sudie had her mind on something Brenda had said earlier in the day. Brenda and Sudie were inseparable from the time Brenda's mother remarried and brought the seven-year-old to live with her Grandma Banks across the road from Sudie's family home. Though the friendship was life-long, the two women's lives could hardly have been more different. The never-married Brenda went on to college and graduate school, finally becoming a magazine editor in New York City, while Sudie never even went to high school and became a wife and mother of four on Bee Branch. Brenda always asks the durndest questions, Sudie thought. Why today Brenda'd asked Sudie how she had been able to make a seemingly happy life out of a shotgun marriage.

Even as Sudie recalled Brenda's question, Brenda sat looking across at the long-married couple and scribbled her recollection of today's conversations on a yellow legal pad, writing out the dialogue between her and her old friend:

"So what's your secret, Sudie?" Brenda began.

"Ain't no secret to it, honey. As I see it, when you get something you get what you get, whether it's what you thought you wanted or not. In the world of picking and choosing I did not pick out Tilt Butcher as my dream man to spend my life with but that's what I got. Me and you both know how I got him and that if I had a' known what I was choosing at the time, he probably woulda been the very last 'n I'd picked— even then. But, as you well know, I was just a kid. He got me in trouble, and we made the best of it. The good Lord knows that's as true for now as it was for then. I didn't set out to have all them youngun's either, but I got 'em and I love every one of 'em to death.

"And, as for Tilt, I reckon I love him too, though I don't tell him so but maybe once in a coon's age—and never in front of anybody else. We're not that kind of people, me and Tilt. As for him loving me, if he's ever said it outright, I never heard it. But now you just take day before yesterday; I was looking out the kitchen window and saw him a'climbing up that steep bank behind the house. I wondered what he was doing cause it was the hottest day and scrambling up that bank wasn't something you'd want to be doing unless you had to. Well, he went outta sight into the woods and a little while later, I saw him making his way back down the same bank with a fistful of the prettiest flowers—you can see 'em in there on the kitchen table in that little blue pitcher.

"Now Tilt knows that my flower garden's 'bout give out——except for them old zinnias, which I don't much like (don't know why I plant 'em even). I mean, there he was a' slippy-sliding down that bank—that big old man a' holding them little flowers in his hand and I just had to laugh out loud. Now, Brennie, Tilt Butcher ain't never gonna write me no love poems, but he loves me and I know that true."

"But do you love him, Sudie—since you didn't choose him, I mean? And if you think you do, how do you know?"

"Well, we've had some good times together, me and Tilt. We laugh a lot about things that happens, and stuff people gets themselves into, and just everyday foolishness—the kids and all."

"But…."

"Wait; that's part of it. But you remember how bad I've

always wanted to see the ocean? Well, for the past fifteen years or so, Mama and Daddy—and Sister, before she left home—have been going to Virginia Beach the first week in July. The first five years, they outright begged us to pick up and go with them—said they'd pay for the room and gas and everything. Now, Brennie, you well know I would have purely loved to go 'specially when the kids where little. Mama and Daddy would've enjoyed being with the grandbabies, the kids would've had a big time playing on the beach. What's more, it would've given me and Tilt both a chance to see the ocean.

"The problem is that I knew full well we couldn't afford to do it on our own—without Daddy paying—and I knew it would hurt Tilt's manhood to have to go on Daddy's money. So, every time it came up, I just claimed that I couldn't take a week away from my garden in July till finally Mama and Daddy just stopped asking and that was that. I druther never see the ocean than to hurt my husband's feelings and I reckon that—more'n any of the good times we've had together— that right there tells me that my heart, for good or bad, is with Tilt Butcher. I don't know when or how it come to be that way, but that's the way it is."

CONNECTED
by Christina St. Clair

"You must come," Katy said, determination in her voice. I knew that she was not going to give in easily.

How could I say no, tell her that I was too hurt from my divorce to be good company, that I was struggling with my identity? I did not want to be a burden. "I don't feel much like driving all that way," I said lamely.

"Eastern Kentucky isn't all that far," she responded. "And it would be good for you to be with other writers. This is a great conference. You have to come!"

"You and Lorn will have a great time without me," I said helplessly. "I need to be alone."

"That is exactly what you don't need," she retorted. "You are coming!"

"You have to promise not to hook me up with a man again," I said to my friend who had arranged three blind dates for me in the past.

"Never! I promise! We are going to share words and get rest and have fun. You will feel at home in the Appalachians. Trust me. This is a wonderful place to go and be with people just as crazy as us. They're all writers!"

"All right," I said, not knowing why I'd agreed. "I will come, but no blind dates!"

"One thing," she said, and her voice was full of laughter, "There are a lot of poets at this conference and you'd better leave them alone! Martin was a saint compared to them! They're a moody, temperamental lot! Do not run with the poets!"

"Fat chance!" I said, choking back tears at the mention of my ex-husband. I forced myself to smile.

Three weeks later, we picked our friend, Lorn, up at Greater Pittsburgh Airport. What with a layover in Atlanta, her flight from Houston had taken about five hours, but she wasn't a bit tired. Her pretty face, always perfectly made up, sparkled with excitement.

"I'm so glad you decided to come," she said to me as we hugged. "This is going to be fun!"

"Yep," I said. "I want it to be." And I did—for them—but I doubted if I'd be particularly happy. I was too wounded, too depressed. As to sharing words and being with writers, that seemed meaningless to me right now. I could only hope my love of writing eventually would return.

I took the back seat of Katy's old land-rover where I would be out of the way. Before long we were bouncing down I-79 into West Virginia. Katy and Lorn chattered eagerly about their latest writing projects, their families, their lives. Their joy at being in each others' company, happy to share the open road of the writer's life, a life that had brought us together, could not help but make me smile a little. I stared out the window at the mountains of West Virginia racing by, noticing the panoramic green beauty, and wondering where I might go to live now that my marriage had ended and everything that had once seemed so certain in my life was now in flux.

As we drove deeper into Eastern Kentucky, the mountains became lower and somehow denser. Small houses and trailers were tucked into every hollow: some beautifully kept, others a shamble of neglect. I wondered what sort of lives these people of Appalachia lived. I did not feel sorry for their poverty any more than I felt sorry for myself. I had not been able to fathom the heart of a man I'd known for most of my life, so who was I to judge the state of a person's house.

The Settlement School where the conference was to be held looked tranquil and safe, a little oasis from the world, nestled between compact old mountains. It was on the outskirts of a tiny town. The most significant place there was the gas station which also sold groceries, burgers, and coffee. It was a hangout for local people. We were far from shopping malls, far from everywhere. I liked the isolation.

At the registration desk, the conference director, Robby, a Kentuckian with a slow way of talking but sharp observant eyes, gave us workshop schedules. "You'll have to sign up to help do the dishes," he said amicably.

Katy grinned at him. "Be glad to," she said. "Provided you give us a good room!"

He scowled then, but looked at his guest list. "You're in the Manor," he said. "Room two on the bottom floor."

Katy's face lit up and she looked like she might throw her arms around him and hug him.

He backed up a step. "You can take your car up there and unload, but then you have to bring it back to the parking lot behind the cafeteria."

"Come on, girls, let's go!"

As soon as I saw the manor, I understood why Katy had been so pleased. It was an ancient wooden farmhouse with a tin roof and a sagging porch, but it was warm and homey.

Inside, I was delighted to find polished wooden floors

and freshly-painted walls adorned with wildlife paintings. All the bedrooms, and I judged there to be four downstairs, led into a central room, dominated by a large stone fireplace that was surrounded by an assortment of rocking chairs, some painted, some wicker.

I found, in spite of my grief, that I was glad to be here with my good friends.

Our room was small but clean. Katy rushed in and threw herself on the double bed next to the window. "I get this one," she said.

"I'd sleep with you," Lorn said playfully, "but I know you snore!" Then she looked at me and politely asked, "Do you mind if I take the top bunk? I'm a little claustrophobic."

"That's fine," I said. I didn't care where I slept.

But, tired though I was from the long drive, I could not sleep. I tossed and turned and my mind raced. At last, in the middle of the night, afraid my restlessness would wake my friends, I crept into the central living room. Every step I took made the old wooden floor creak and I held my breath, fearful I would wake the strangers who were hidden behind the doors of the other bedrooms. How many women slept in this house tonight, I did not know, but I did not want to meet any of them. I sat for a while, alone, with only the dim rays of the hall night-light reflecting on an old picture of a woodcock. It might have been an original engraving, perhaps a priceless treasure, but all I saw were dead feathers and lifeless eyes.

At last, I crept back to the bedroom and tugged the door shut, but it wouldn't latch. The dim light from the hallway radiated into the room. I was sure the door had been locked before and I could not understand what was preventing it from shutting now. If one door closes, another opens, I thought, and anxiety made me want to laugh, but all I could do was stand silently tugging on the handle.

Then suddenly there was a squeaking, crying sound, and my arms turned into lumps of jelly. I thought I had trapped a mouse. With dread I fumbled for the light switch. Oh how I hated to find anything that I might have hurt! How I hated to be the perpetrator of pain! And how very afraid I was!

There between the edge of the door and the door jam was a baby bird, a fledgling who could not even fly yet. I stood there frozen, staring at the poor little creature. Katy groaned at the bright light, then clambered out of her cozy double bed. Quickly and gently she picked up the little bird and cradled it in the palm of her hand and warmed it. The creature did not seem badly injured. It lay passively, its feathers quivering, its heart beating wildly, and its eyes staring but alive.

Lorn yelled from the top bunk, "Turn the light out!" And she hunkered back under the covers and did not budge.

Katy and I took the little bird into the living room and looked up the chimney of the stone fireplace, hoping we might find a nest. The chimney was tall and if the bird had come into the house that way, there was no way to send it back up the dark opening: it was too young to fly. We thought about putting it on the ground next to the tree beside the house and hoping the mother-bird would come for it, but when we went outside, it seemed too dark and too wild. We feared our little bird would be prey for cats and foxes and who knew what. So we went back into the house and put the little creature in a shoe box and wrapped it in a towel to keep it warm until morning when we could decide what to do with it.

As Katy turned out the light, she said to me, "I'm not sure what kind of bird it is, but I think it might be a purple martin. No wonder you slammed it in the door!" She grinned, amused at her clever reference to my estranged husband, Martin. Perhaps it was funny, to her. But my mind went immediately to my former husband and to the misery of my divorce. I lay the rest of the night thinking how lost and hurt and tiny, unconscious of the repercussions of his actions, my husband Martin had been.

The next morning when we went outside, we could see people gathering in the valley below us, welcoming one another and chatting eagerly. Overwhelmed by my need for solitude, I told my friends to go ahead of me. I could not face such a mass of thoughts and words. I sat down on a rough-hewn wooden bench on the grassy hill above the proceedings and watched all those people engaged in the business of being together. The sun was shining and the August air was already sultry and hot. Perspiration dampened my forehead. I did not move. I sat, glad to be alone, and watched these people who seemed to be swollen with expectation, pregnant to begin the newness of this week, but I felt unable to join in.

Yet there was comfort in that valley below me where all those people raised excited voices together in a communion of like-spirit. I felt hope as well as the pain of my separateness: here were all these people who loved words, not unlike me. They too had secret hurts, secret wishes, abandoned friendships, lost lovers, new beginnings. But, in my insecurity I thought, they are all masters of words and I am the only apprentice here, just as I am an apprentice in life. How can I, a failure at marriage, and woefully unpublished, ever enter into this community of masters?

Katy came panting up the hill, her face beaming with excitement. "The conference director's son said he can raise our baby bird until she's ready to spread her wings. He thinks she'll survive."

I smiled as warmly as my heart would allow, not wanting to drag my friend down by my disconnected state.

"I was just coming," I said.

"Good," Katy responded. "You are going to have such a great time here. I can't wait to see J.W. Last year we slugged back a bottle of whiskey together. Or rather he did. That's too much booze for me, but he is an incredible teacher and will make you love Appalachian literature. I want you to hear him. Come on! Come to breakfast!"

As Katy led me to the dining hall, I thought how words can be daggers or caresses, used for good or ill, communications of so much more than mere sounds formed by the mouth, the tongue, the throat, and the breath. I remembered the words my husband had used that had changed my life forever, words that plunged me into despair.

I found a tray and followed Katy down the line, taking meager portions of scrambled eggs, a strip of bacon, a piece of toast. All these people made me nervous. I was on my own now.

I was out in the world without an anchor.

"There's J.W.," Katy said and pointed to a long table full of noisy people. There was only one vacant place.

"You go ahead. I'll be fine. Go on, go!"

Katy grinned and hurried over to the large group who were laughing and joking, gobbling up ham and eggs, slurping coffee. I envied them, these free people, these writer-people.

I chose a smaller table where three less talkative individuals sat: two men and a woman.

Almost as soon as I settled down, the woman excused herself, and I found myself alone with the two men. I was aware of my availability, and I looked at these two men and wondered about them. Not that I wanted a man. Not now. It was too soon. I was too vulnerable, too wounded. Perhaps later there would be relationships.

The talk was of books and literature.

"Some writer I once heard insisted everyone ought to read *Moby Dick* or else they couldn't call themselves writers," I said. "I tried. I couldn't get through it. The words were good. The style was good. But it was slow and dark and I had no interest in plodding through all that stuff. It seems to me we don't retain anything unless it engages our minds and hearts."

The men nodded, and one of them finished his coffee, got up and left. I sat, aware of being alone with the other man, and I looked at him and wondered who he really was beneath the veneer of superficial conversation. His fierce face and his untrimmed beard did not invite intimacy, but his eyes, intense and arrogant, looked at me steadily, trying to fathom me. And I knew that I was as aloof as he was, but that we were somehow forming a connection.

When he stood up to leave, he seemed to unwind and rise to the ceiling. I'd never particularly liked tall men, but his stature was commanding, and I felt my own tallness complemented. I felt feminine again.

Later when most people were at workshops or getting manuscripts critiqued, I came across him sitting outside. "So," I said, looking at him scribbling notes on a page, "what do you write?"

Silently, he handed me the page he'd been working on. I remained standing and read his words, and I felt as though I'd been handed a promise. It was as if his literature was his covenant of honor. I read quietly. Those words so skillfully crafted on the page conveyed to me more than all the chatter and small talk we could possibly hope to engage in during one year, let alone a few days. In his lines I felt sincerity, pain, humor, cynicism, love, irony and awareness. I was astounded and impressed. I felt I already knew him.

"Join me," he suggested and motioned to a wicker rocking chair next to him.

I eased into the seat, feeling shy but exhilarated. He said little, while I chattered about my life, telling him far more than I ought, but he sat quietly in his chair listening, smoking cigarette after cigarette, watching me keenly. I did not mind. His lack of words felt like a sea of compassion, long-lasting, allowing my words to float, to dive, to resurface with new meaning, the meaning that comes from having been heard.

Katy, Lorn and I sat together at dinner. It was the first time I'd seen them since lunch. Country ham, brown bean soup, corn bread, spiced apple rings and green beans sat lovingly on my plate. The dining room hummed with happy voices. A man Katy met in a children's writers' workshop plopped down at our table. He talked politely with Katy, but his eyes stared hungrily at Lorn's pretty face. She saw his look. I stifled a giggle. The minute he left, she raised her eyebrows at me. "We want to know every detail," she said and began to grin like a school girl.

"Yeah," Katy said. "We saw you in, shall we say, heated discussion with the same guy you had breakfast with. Out with it. Who is he?"

"I can only tell you this," I said and folded my arms primly across my chest. "He is a quiet man, rather conservative!"

"Come on," they cajoled. "We see your eyes sparkling!"

"So?" I replied evasively. "What does that mean?"

"Nothing, unless he's after you. He is, isn't he?"

Katy interrupted. "He's not married, is he? Don't get involved with a married man!"

"I won't. He's not anyway," I said.

"Is he experienced?" Lorn asked.

All I could do was laugh. Over her shoulder I saw him enter the dining room. "I'll be right back." I hurried over to him.

"Hi," I said. "After dinner, would you like to go for a walk?"

His eyes lit up and he nodded yes.

"Meet you in about twenty minutes outside the door." Then I rejoined Katy and Lorn who were trying to hide their faces so I couldn't see them tittering.

Katy bounced upright in her chair. "He's not! Tell me, he's not!"

"Not what?" Lorn asked and leaned towards me scrutinizing my face.

I looked away. Laughter rose up inside me.

"Not what?" Lorn persisted.

"A poet, Lorn."

"Tell me he isn't a poet!" Katy said.

"I can't." I looked at my watch. "I have to go now. I have a date."

We walked into the village.

A young man, black from coal dust, stared at us, his bright eyes blazing from his sooty face. My heart ached for him. I wished he had more choices than to spend a life underground. My life, I thought, was not so different from his: in many ways I had lived in the darkness too.

We crossed the street and wandered up a gravel road and came into an old cemetery. Grass grew in tangles around the crumbling tombstones. Patches of wild daises gleamed in the sunlight. Sweat ran down our faces. He took my hand and we strolled around, trying not to tread on the graves.

"Look," I said. "There are three little children buried here. And this must be the mother and father. How sad. The whole family must have been wiped out by disease."

He looked at me thoughtfully, then put his arm around me.

I rested my head against his shoulder and we stood together, side by side, looking at the weathered markers: no longer sharp-edged but rounded, with moss spreading over their uneven surfaces.

Just beyond the family graves I noticed a wild orchid, purple and delicate. It was all I could do not to run to the flower and kneel to see if it was fragrant, but I remained quiet, saying nothing. The promise of his arm touching mine warmed me. I did not want to spoil this moment.

We lingered for a while then slowly made our way back to the Settlement School. He walked me to my house. We sat on a bench on the porch, our arms wrapped about each other. He told me of his life, how he'd been writing poetry since he was a boy; how poetry was his passion. He told me how much he enjoyed teaching the people of Eastern Kentucky, whose origins were the same as his. His people had been farmers, lumberjacks and mill workers, not much different from the coal miners and tobacco growers of this area. And not much different from my parents who had worked long hard hours, denying themselves, in order to raise me and my brothers.

I trusted this man. I liked him. When he drew me close and kissed me, my heart fluttered like the little martin's, not out of fear or pain or entrapment, but with hope, pleasure, and the promise of a future.

In the morning he came to my door with a bouquet of wild purple flowers, perhaps not as showy as the orchid in the cemetery, but more splendid because he had discerned my love for nature. We gazed into one another's eyes and walked outside and stood under the tree next to the bedroom window.

"I know someone with a great townhouse," he said, a twinkle in his eye. "What say we blow this conference and go there?"

"Yes," I said. This man knew I loved purple flowers, this man knew I loved words, and this man knew how to hold my hand and kiss me. "Yes!" I said again. This man and I were soul-mates.

Suddenly the window flew open. "I told you not to run with the poets!" Katy yelled with a big smile on her face.

"I know," I said. "But I can't help myself."

That afternoon we eloped to his townhouse.

A Matter of Perspective
by Alexandra Combs Hudson

Shocked, Clifford White read the obituary again with his fist pressed tightly over his mouth. His breakfast coffee and a half smoked cigarette sat forgotten. He rose, walked to the window, and looked out over the valley through moist eyes. It was hard to know what he felt just at that moment. He remembered how it had been when his wife had died three years ago.

He had loved her in his own way, and they had been loyal and supportive of each other, but she had known she had not been the love of his life.

His mind flooded with youthful memories of a beautiful dark-haired girl with vivid blue eyes. They had been in love, but her father and mother had forbidden them to see each other again. He was never sure why. But she had given in, and they had both gone on to marry someone else. They had raised their families, seldom speaking to each other at all over the years. He had seen her, recently, crossing the street in town. She was tall and slim, as lovely as ever.

But he had not dared to even think about this, for fear God would damn him to hell for wishing death on someone. It wasn't like when he was in the army, and you gritted your teeth and killed whatever got in your way, just to survive. This would have been a murderous thought against a peaceful and unarmed man. Yet here it was in black and white, and he felt guilty.

His heart went out to her with all that was in him, and he ached to comfort her, but he knew he could not. It was too soon. She and her children needed time to hold each other and grieve. He would not attend the funeral. There was too much to think through. He went to the table, lit another cigarette, and refilled his coffee cup.

•••

The phone by the kitchen door rang and Rebecca Conley dried her hands, stepped into the living room, and picked up the receiver. "Hello?" She nearly dropped the receiver when she heard the voice on the other end.

"Beck?" Clifford's voice shook. "This is Clifford White. Are you all right?"

"I nearly dropped the phone! I didn't expect to ever hear from you again!"

"Well, I just wanted to see how you were getting along. I was sorry to hear that John had died."

"Well, I'm glad you thought about me."

"Yeah, I was remembering how hard it was when my wife died three years ago."

"Yes, I remember. Have you been all right since then?"

"Oh, yeah, I've done pretty well. Being alone again takes some getting used to, but it's been O.K. But I've worried a lot about you lately, and I decided to call. Look, how 'bout I stop by this afternoon and we can talk about old times."

"O.K., that sounds great! I'll be glad to see you again!" She hung up the phone and sat down abruptly in an overstuffed chair. "Wow!" She thought, fanning weakly. And then she thought some more, and hugged those thoughts to herself. She had not allowed herself to think about him in that way since her marriage 40 years ago. It amazed her that her thoughts and feelings were as strong as they had been when she was a teenager. Then she realized that it wasn't a dream, that he really was coming, and she flew into action. She glanced around the room to see what needed to be done. It was OK there, and the dishes were done. There was coffee and homemade pie—but her hair was a mess!

She rushed to the bathroom, showered, and washed her hair. She went through half her closet while her hair dried. Finally she found just the right casual-but-not-too-casual outfit. Up went her hair onto hot rollers, and on went her makeup. Her hands flew. She made final adjustments to slacks and hair as the doorbell rang. It was all she could do not to race to the front door. She walked slowly across the room and let the doorbell ring a second time as she tried to calm her racing heart.

•••

Clifford hoped that she wasn't upset that he had called. He pushed the doorbell again. She hadn't sounded upset—just surprised. The door swung open and his answer glowed in her face. Dark hair shone, blue eyes sparkled, and she could not have stopped the welcoming smile if she had wanted to. His smile answered hers as she closed the door behind him.

•••

"Mother! You've ruined my life!" Leigh Ann burst into tears and ran into her old bedroom. Rebecca heard the lock click, and felt tears sting her eyes. She had known this would be difficult, but this was worse than she had expected. Her sons had accepted the revelation that she would be dating someone, almost as if they had expected it. But their baby sister, for all her thirty years, was going to take a long time to come around. She let the subject drop for now. She had learned a little about the grieving process in the two years since her husband had died, and she felt sure this reaction was part of it. Leigh Ann still felt the need to protect her father's memory.

Rebecca reached for the phone. "Cliff?"

"Yes."

"I told them. The boys are fine, but Leigh Ann is throwing a pure fit. How did your kids take it?"

"My boys took it fine. I didn't think they'd have any trouble, and they didn't."

"Well, we'll have to give Leigh Ann time. I hope she'll come around. I don't think I can stand it if she keeps this up."

"Beck, you can't throw me over again, just because your kid doesn't like the idea." His voice rose. "She might as well get used to the idea that she's not the boss any more. Now you listen to me! I can't stand it if you do that again!" He controlled himself with great effort. "I'll call you back later, Beck", he said in a muffled voice. He really wouldn't be able to stand it if it happened again.

Rebecca went to her own room, flung herself on the bed and cried. It hurt her to think that she might have hurt him again. She remembered how for years after their forced breakup she had cried every time anyone mentioned his name. By the time her mother had relented it was too late, and he had married someone else. She knew then that she couldn't lose him again. Leigh Ann would just have to get over it. They could give her time. They could do that much.

Rebecca got up, washed her face, and made a pot of coffee. She sat by the phone with her cup in hand, and dialed Clifford White's phone number. There was no answer.

Rebecca forced down the panic. Somehow this was all her fault. She walked slowly, mechanically to the kitchen and began preparing Sunday dinner. The boys were stopping by, and they would be hungry. She wasn't hungry.

•••

Clifford walked out of the house and up the mountain to the beech flat. It was peaceful there, and he had to calm himself. Lighting a cigarette, he sat down on his favorite tree stump. He had thought he was stronger than that, and felt ashamed. He felt as if he had failed Beck, and placed blame on her that he had not intended. He knew he would not see her until tomorrow, and it would be a long, lonely wait. He watched the sun touch the mountain range and headed quickly home before it went completely dark.

Back in his warm bright kitchen, he fixed a can of chicken noodle soup and a ham sandwich for supper. The warm food was comforting. He lit a cigarette, stretched his feet out toward the electric heater, and turned on the television. The phone rang.

•••

"Hello", he said sleepily.

"Cliff, where've you been?" Rebecca asked. "I was worried to death because you were so upset! I've been nearly crazy trying to rush the kids out of here so I could call you back! I called a while ago, and you didn't answer. Where were you?"

"I just walked up the mountain a little ways to the beech flat. I'm sorry about a while ago. I didn't mean to lose it, but I meant what I said. What are you going to do?"

"We'll have to give her time, Cliff."

"How much time are we talking about? Can I see you while we're giving her 'time'? If this isn't going to work out, we need to stop it now before it gets any harder. I don't think I can stand to lose you now, as it is." He was getting upset again. "Tell me something, for God's sake!"

"Cliff, I can't stand to lose you again, either! Please don't get upset again! It's going to be OK, and we can see each other, just not around Leigh Ann for a while."

Relief flooded him. "Can I come over right now, just for a minute? I need to touch you, to hold you, to see in your eyes that you mean it."

"I mean it, and no, you can't come over. You have to wait until tomorrow", she said firmly. "I'm dead tired, and I can't deal with any more tonight. I'm too old for this kind of thing. I'll see you tomorrow." She hung up as he opened his mouth and spoke to an empty line.

"Well, now, isn't that just like a woman!" He thumped the phone down with irritation. He sighed and turned the television back up. He was as drained as she had been.

The next day Clifford asked for and received permission to take Rebecca to lunch in town. He arrived at eleven thirty, and she let him in, looking tired and strained. He took her in his arms and they held each other for a long time.

"Are you OK?" he asked at last.

"I'm OK", she answered.

"Let's go, then." She got her jacket, and they got into his black pickup truck and headed for town.

"The Mountain Mama Restaurant OK?" He asked. She

nodded. There wasn't a lot to choose from in a small town, but the Mountain Mama made delicious home-style meals. They ordered fried chicken, potato salad, peas, and rolls, and both ate as if they hadn't eaten in three days. Then they finished up with turtle cheesecake and coffee, laughing at each other for being such gluttons. She watched him smoke a cigarette, enjoying the masculine scent of the tobacco as the smoke curled and rose about him. It was good to see him relax. Feeling much better as they left the restaurant, they waved happily at two friends on the street outside.

Rebecca waited in the truck while Cliff ran into True Value Hardware for nails. He had promised to do some repairs to her back porch. They were both anxious to get back. They enjoyed their time doing chores together, whether at his house or hers, and there was a lot of work to keeping two homes going. They were both thinking about that as they drove to Rebecca's house in a comfortable silence.

Hours later, their work done and a light supper eaten, they sat side by side on the sofa watching TV. He put his arm around her, and she laid her head on his shoulder. "Beck" he said, "I want to ask you something."

"Yes?"

"You know I've always loved you."

"I know. And I love you."

He knew she meant it, and he felt confident. "I want you to marry me, and I'd like it to be soon."

"I'm not ready to get married quite yet. Even if Leigh Ann was OK, I'd still have to have some time to get used to the idea." She sounded unusually coquettish, and he glanced at her suspiciously. Just what did that woman have on her mind? He'd never known her to be much of a thinking woman—but she was thinking about something, and he wasn't at all sure he liked it.

•••

She thought about what he had asked her. He wanted to get married as quickly as possible. She guessed he was afraid he would lose her, but she was sure that was not going to happen. So what was it that suddenly made her hesitant?

She knew the emotional stress of the last few days was not something she wanted to repeat. She really didn't remember having such an emotionally rough time since their breakup years ago. That was one thing that she had found to be a blessing in her marriage. It had had very little of this kind of emotional turmoil. Her husband had left her alone to go her own way as long as she took care of the kids, the house, the financial management and, occasionally, his physical needs. She had enjoyed the hard work, and the kids. She had enjoyed the control of finances, and the freedom to go when and where she liked. And, ten years her senior, he had been a gentle lover. She had loved him for his gentleness.

Suddenly, she knew why she hesitated, and she raised one eyebrow and smiled quizzically at herself. It was all a matter of perspective. This man would want to be underfoot all the time, and she needed some personal freedom. Still, she wanted him, and she wanted him to want her. But this was a different wanting from that of a teenage girl. She was her own person now, and she knew she could get along fine on her own. She had her husband's retirement income, and that gave her a certain amount of freedom. She still wanted her own space, and she was going to have it. He would just have to accept that. They would work things out as they went along. They both loved to travel, and to do their chores together.

They would learn the best way to deal with it over time.

•••

Cliff walked to his living room window and looked out over the valley. He pictured what his own obituary would say. 'Clifford White, age 63, died Friday, March 22, 2000, in the Hazard Appalachian Regional Hospital of lung cancer. He is survived by three sons, one brother, two sisters, and a host of nieces and nephews. His funeral will be held..." he stopped abruptly. He knew what he had to do. He picked up the phone, and dialed Rebecca's number.

"Hello?"

"Beck, I have to talk to you. I'll be there in an hour."

"OK" was all she had time to say. He had hung up the phone almost before she had finished saying it.

It had been three days since they had sat on the sofa and necked. She couldn't imagine what had happened, but something sure had. She had just finished fixing her hair and make-up when the doorbell rang. Looking up into his serious, determined face, she saw something that made her breath die away. He took her by the shoulders, and pushing her gently inside, closed the door behind them.

"Beck, you've got a decision to make today."

"What?" She gasped. "I thought..."

"Well, things have changed. The medical tests I had done last week have come back positive. I have lung cancer in my left lung. The doctor said we caught it early, but there will still have to be surgery and chemotherapy. He says my chances are good, but if the surgery and treatment don't get it, then I'll be dead in less than a year. I know you won't accept anything less than marriage, but it's not fair to ask you to marry a man with a death sentence hanging over his head.

I'm just asking if you will be there for me or not, and asking you to tell me now. There just isn't any more time to give Leigh Ann, or to think about it ourselves. I have surgery on Monday, and I need to know."

Rebecca was crying openly now, and he took her in his arms.

"Oh, no! Oh, no!" was all she could say as she clung to him.

"Look at me." Clifford tilted her chin back to look into her anguished, tear-filled eyes. "We have five days. And I love you."

"And I love you," she answered. "And I'll marry you. Today."

"Yes, my darling."

Their lips met and clung as though nothing would ever part them again. Not fear, not sorrow, not death itself.

EVELYN ALICE WAS A FARM WOMAN
by Kate Larken

Evelyn Alice was a farm woman. She was born on a farm, grew up on a farm, married Burl and moved from her daddy's farm to his to live for the next thirty-five, forty years.

Evelyn Alice was a farm woman through and through. She loved it—not so much the typical role of being a farm wife, but the farming itself. Now, honey, you came up farming; you can testify how it'll kind of get into your blood, whether you want it to or not. (What in the world has gotten into this corn meal? Oh my heart, is that a weevil?) Well, anyway, that's the way it was with Evelyn Alice. She'd get out there and work alongside Burl in the beans and corn and piglot. She'd pull a calf just the same as any farmer, and she'd drive a tractor, pitch and stack bales, auger grain, butcher a hog. (Hand that strainer over here to me, will you?) You know how most farm wives are usually thought of as the one that cooks for the work crews that come in for hay or harvest? Well, she did that—but she was part of the crew, too.

Truth be known, the reason Burl married her in the first place was because she was known as such a good hand on the farm. He thought she was kind of plain to look at, but since he didn't plan on looking at her all that much, it didn't matter to him. (My stars in heaven, I can't believe I'm tellin' you all of this. Honey, have you seen my good cake plate?) Well, anyway. Anyway. He upped and married her, and figured he'd got a pretty good bargain, as farmers, being fiscally conservative types by nature and necessity, like to think they usually do. Old boys like Burl aren't ever surprised when they strike a good bargain—they expect it. No bargain, no sale. It's something about agrarian prowess, I reckon. At least that's what Evelyn Alice always said. She was a firecracker, that Evelyn Alice was.

What did take Burl by surprise, though, is that after living with Evelyn Alice through that first haying season and into combining beans after cold weather set in, he began to think that maybe besides liking her (for the most part) and respecting her agricultural talent (entirely), he guessed maybe he had come to love her after all. And that stunned him a little at first—but later he came to believe that what it was was an outright indicator of just how good he'd come to be at spotting a bargain. Why, he thought he was so good he might ought to be on the TV or something.

Still, Evelyn Alice never let whatever was going on in Burl's head carry too much weight with her. She knew the trade-off right from the start. Figured it out. Knew he had more hired her than married her. Took note, too, when he started to soften a bit toward her after those first few months. But she was pretty indifferent to the whole thing because what he didn't know was that she had only married him as a trade-off for life as a farmer on a place that she could think of at least partly as her own. And she liked Burl fine...always had.

But what Evelyn Alice loved, besides farming, was to hunt.

Nothing suited her more than stomping around a rabbit field or easing through a squirrelly woods early on a crisp, cold morning. Best meal in the world to her was a breakfast of pan-fried rabbit or squirrel with gravy and biscuits. Now, honey, you grew up eating thataway, and you know exactly what I mean about biting down easy so as not to break the fillings out of your jaw teeth on the shot.

So she'd kill it and skin it and cook it up too. She raised a garden and canned. She made their clothes. Strung barbed wire, ran a corn picker and organized the meetings for the 4-H horse project. She could build new things and she could fix broken things.

Evelyn Alice was what you'd call her own woman.

She and Burl had three or four young-uns…I can't remember now, but it was either three or four. Boys and girls both. Oh and when it came to her children, now she had a heavy hand with the loving and a light touch with the discipline. But you know, not a one of those kids was spoiled, and they ever' one turned out to be the nicest most wonderful young adults ever was. Just "no, ma'am" and "yes, ma'am" and "thank you, ma'am" all over the place…and mean it, too. And then Evelyn Alice became a mamaw, and that just pleased her to no end. Those young'uns of hers all went off and moved away to marry and go to colleges and have their babies and get good jobs, 'course, but they left an impression on me, I'll tell you. "How you this morning, ma'am?" I just mean to tell you, now.

For the most part, all those years they worked separate from one another, Evelyn Alice and Burl. What I mean by that is he'd maybe be feeding the calves while she was over yonder tilling the garden plot. Or she'd be in the back yard fixing the clothesline post while he was out by the crib shucking corn. 'Course, now, when it came to fencing or getting in hay or canning, they did those things together. But the rest of the time they were like all other farm couples; one worked here while the other worked there. Not too different from the way couples go to work at different places these days, except Burl and Evelyn Alice ate ever' meal together and were at least working on the same project…their farm and the life they led there.

But funny thing: once the raising of the offspring was pretty much done, Evelyn Alice and Burl got to feeling particularly close to one another in their later years. You'd see 'em doing things together around the place. They'd even sit side by side on the front porch, rocking slow, fo'rd and back'rd, in that blue metal glider after the early news and weather went off. They started listening to one another after all those years. He said sweet things he never intended to say. And she said things back that she never thought she could.

(Would you turn down the eye under those potatoes? Thank you, honey. Your beans could use a stir.)

The way it happened was the most odd thing that ever was. It was one of those nice spring days, not too hot, where they had things pretty much caught up (at least as caught up as they can ever be on a farm) and Burl said, "Why don't you come ride with me a while," meaning on the tractor. He had broken new ground shortly before and had just about finished disking it up for the second time. Had a few more rounds to go and thought it might be nice to have Evelyn Alice ride along while he finished it. They'd done and eaten dinner, watched the noon news, listened to the hog market and the grain futures, and it occurred to him that they had the whole afternoon, or at least this first part of it, to be out under the sky together making the ground ready for growing.

Evelyn Alice took one look at the dishes still settin' on the tabletop and thought, "I ought to do these nasty dishes before I do another thing," and then said, "Just for a little while," which made Burl's face crack into that leathery smile she liked and didn't see often enough.

So they went. He was using their little Ford redbelly tractor to pull the disc. You know that old disc of your granddaddy's out yonder behind the milking shed? The one with weeds growing up through it that he's not used in ages? It was like that—rows and rows of them sharp metal wheels that slice and dice the dirt 'til it's fine enough to plant. Well, they were rolling along, cutting up clods, and everything was going fine. Sky was a pretty pale blue with fluffy white clouds like off of a picture postcard. They chugged along on the redbelly, stirring up a breeze. Burl drove and Evelyn Alice sat up on the fender to his left. I saw them out there as I passed by on McGee Springs Road, right there near Reece Corner where their place butts up against the old schoolhouse line. I was on my way to the post office or the store or somewhere—beauty shop, I think —and I thought, "Well, will wonders never cease?" For there they both were, him discing and her perched up on that fender like a decoration.

It wasn't until I got to the post office—that's right, I must have been headed for the beauty shop when I saw 'em because it was probably two hours before I got done there, and then was when I went by the post office. Well, anyway, it wasn't until I got to the post office window that I found out about it, but I reckon it must have happened right after I'd passed by their place.

Ever'body knows it's dangerous to ride on the fender of a tractor, but we've all done it and do it still. Who would have thought the old fender was so rusty it would just give away like that?

He was looking back over his right shoulder, like they do, and didn't realize at first what it was. That left fender just broke all of a sudden—dumped her forward off the tractor, right in front of the big back tire. Well, it ran her over, but that wouldn't have been the worst thing in the world because the ground was so soft from where he had already worked it up pretty good. Plus, we'd had a right smart of rain a day or two before. But then here come the disc.

When a thing like that happens so fast, you just can't react like you want to. And then when you remember it—see it kind of in slow motion—you think you had more time than you actually did.

Burl always will blame himself, no matter what we all tell him. He'll always think it was his fault. He'll always see her covered in dirt and blood and gashed all to pieces and hurting so bad. He'll always scream inside of his head that he's to blame—if only he'd known the fender mount was bad, if only he'd known she was falling before she hit, if only he'd been looking over his left shoulder instead of his right.

Well, can't anything in this world be done about it now but just remember. (Here, honey, set this bread on the table.) I think about it ever' now and then, and here's what I've come to believe:

There's things in this world worse than dying into your own soil. You can be overseas fighting somebody else's fight; you can be lying on cold concrete, coughing 'til you can't breathe no more; you can wrap yourself all the way around a tree in twisted metal and rusty chrome; you can be by yourself and miserable and wasting away with only strangers nearby to hope for help from.

But hers come to her better than that, Lord love her.

I expect that in those last moments of her life, Evelyn Alice was just about the happiest she'd ever been—with dirty dishes in the sink and doing something so romantic and impulsive as riding on the fender of her husband's tractor on a perfect spring day.

Evelyn Alice was, after all, a farm woman.

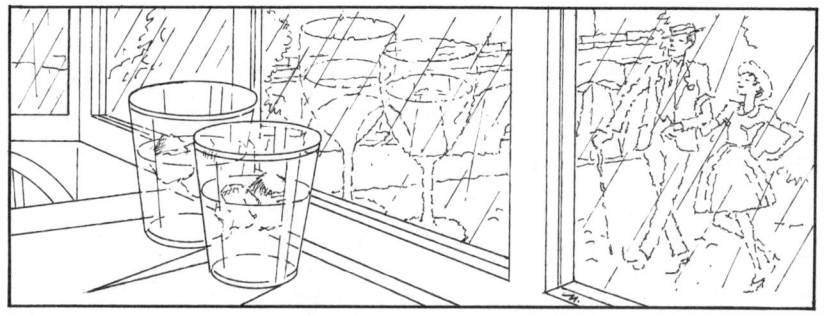

ON THE LEFT BANK
by Barbara Smith

What else was there to do? Lorraine had straightened
her tiny room, so tiny there was hardly space to bend over to
touch her toes, even if she still could, so tiny that if she
stood next to her bed and reached sideways, she could probably touch both walls at the same time. It was so tiny that the
closet would hold only four dresses or two skirts and maybe
three blouses, but that was o.k. It didn't matter if she wore
the same outfits over and over, just so they were clean. The
worst part was that there was no place for her books except
on the floor of her closet, next to her two pairs of shoes,
and large-print books.

They wouldn't even let her put pictures on the walls.
Freshly painted, they said, but Lorraine knew better. Crouch-
ing, she had seen the heel marks near the floor, the bare spots
where someone had tried to scour stains from around the
door. Still, no pictures allowed. She could not have seen them
anyhow, but at least she would have known that the blue and
green blurs inside the fuzzy frames were her own blue and
green blurs. She would be able to look at them and remember her West Virginia roots: Blackwater Falls in May, the
dogwood trees on the hill behind her house, her used-to-be

house in Rainelle.

What else was there to do? There was no point in turning on the TV—the wall-mounted screen was only another blur, and there weren't many programs that were worth listening to without being able to see the pictures, except for the news. Katie Couric and Matt Lauer kept her company, but their news was so depressing—Iraq, Bosnia, Taiwan, Los Angeles. And if any of the attendants caught her watching such sad stuff, they turned the TV to some stupid game show. She peered at her oversized watch, squinted, and guessed it was midafternoon. Oh, how long today was. How long yesterday. How long tomorrow.

The door opened. Lorraine looked up from where she was sitting cross-legged on the bed. "Dr. Lorraine?" the peach-colored blur asked. "Would you like to go for a little walk?" The voice was young and feminine, the figure vague. "Maybe down the hall, maybe the sun room?"

"Solarium," Lorraine corrected the girl.

"Solarium," The voice seemed to be smiling. "Would you like to?"

"How about outdoors?"

"Not today, Miss Lorraine. Just the solarium."

"Outdoors."

"Maybe later. I'll ask, but it's pretty cold."

"What is the temperature? What month is this?" Lorraine asked.

"There was frost on the ground this morning, and it's Thursday, March 23."

"Yes." Lorraine unfolded her legs, turned to the side of the bed, and let herself down. "Do you see my brown shoes?" Lorraine knew full well that her loafers were lined up neatly next to the books.

The attendant came close, leaned down, and scooted the shoes close. "Can you put them on yourself?" she asked.

"Of course." Lorraine easily slid in her right foot, then her left. "Even my feet have lost weight," she remarked. She tugged at the belt that kept her skirt from falling right off to the floor, then peered at the face now close to her own. "I think I'm getting shorter," she smiled. "How tall are you?"

"Five-seven," the girl said. "How tall are you?"

"I haven't shrunk as much as I thought. I was five-nine once."

"You're still taller than I am."

"Not much."

"At least an inch." The girl took Lorraine's bony elbow, squeezing it lightly. "Come on. Let's walk a little."

"I used to walk five miles every single day after school," Lorraine offered. "Sometimes on Saturdays I'd walk all day. One Saturday I walked all the way from Philippi to Elkins." She laughed. "And then I didn't have any way to get home. I had to call my minister to come get me."

The girl laughed as they moved toward the door. "I'll bet you never did that again."

"No—but I hiked the Appalachian Trail that summer."

They were in the hall, turning right. "The whole trail?" the girl asked.

"No. It takes months to do that." Lorraine smiled. "But I would have if I'd had the time. Now I have the time," Lorraine smiled, "but I've misplaced my hiking boots.

"What kind of perfume are you wearing?" the old woman asked. "I thought they wouldn't allow perfume here."

"I forgot," the girl admitted. "It's called Countdown. My folks gave it to me for Valentine's Day."

"Valentine's Day. The Cub Scouts made favors for us."

"I know. My mom has a den."

"Remind me, dear. Your name?" They were almost at the end of the hall.

"Tess."

"Yes. Like D'Urberville. I should have remembered. She's one of my favorite characters in all British literature," Lorraine said.

"My mom's, too. How do you know about English literature?"

"I taught it for forty-seven years, from age nineteen to age sixty-six. Then I made the mistake of retiring. " Lorraine straightened her shoulders, circling them for a little exercise.

"Mistake? I would think you'd be ready after forty-seven years."

"I thought it would be smart to quit while I could still be active, but now I've outlived everybody but God and a few angels." She looked sideways, quite sure the girl was smiling. "I believe I may be old enough to be your great-great, maybe great-great-great grandmother. Eighty-seven."

"That's wonderful," the girl said.

"A wonder, yes. A wonder as to why God isn't interested in my company yet."

The girl had stopped walking, though she was still holding Lorraine's arm. The tone and volume of her voice dropped. "You want to die?"

"Oh, my goodness, yes. Eighty-seven is too long to live. Eighty-six is plenty." She chuckled. "By the time you're eighty-five, you've lost your family—they've moved away or they're old themselves or they're dead—and you've outlived all your friends, and your tastebuds and your sense of smell and your eyesight have quit in disgust, and your teeth are in the jar more than they're in your mouth, and your money is being enjoyed by doctors and insurance agents."

Tess started walking again, Lorraine's hand tucked inside her elbow. An old man shuffled by, pushing his walker, leaving a trail of the aroma of stale urine and liniment. "That's another thing," Lorraine whispered. "You can stay interested in men as long as they smell good, but, my dear, there comes a point when they're downright disgusting, and you're always afraid that you may be just as repulsive yourself."

"You're not!" Tess insisted."You smell like wildflowers in the spring. Like a meadow when a May breeze blows across it."

"Ha! That's my soap. I hope it lasts." Lorraine sighed. "My one remaining luxury. I'm on my last bar."

"I'll get you more," Tess promised.

They reached the solarium, and Lorraine could sense more than see that there were four or five others there ahead of her. "Where would you like to sit?" Tess asked. "Mrs. Larinsky is over near the window talking to Mrs. Sougher, and Mr. Linkous is sitting by himself playing cards."

"By myself, I think," Lorraine murmured. "Those two women are—"

A crackly voice interrupted her from behind. "Doctor." It sounded like a man. "If you think you can stand the smell of me, I would be delighted to have you join me."

Lorraine could feel Tess turn, and she turned her own head, though she couldn't quite see the speaker.

"It's Mr. Brandt," Tess said loudly.

"Thank you, my dear," Lorraine replied, "but I'm not as deaf as I am blind."

Before the girl could apologize, the man persisted. "Dr. Foster. Join me."

"At what?" the elderly woman asked.

"He's just—" Tess began, but again there was a gentle interruption.

"My first name is Carl," the man said, "and I would enjoy your company."

"How do you know?" Lorraine asked. "I can be a real bitch."

She heard two chuckles, one high-pitched, one low. "I can," she insisted. "Ask my students."

"I'll risk it," Brandt said. "Come on. Join me."

Lorraine felt Tess pulling on her arm. "All right," Lorraine conceded. "You don't have to get nasty. You're all the same," she said to the aide. "Stubborn. Mean."

"Well," said the girl, now taking Lorraine's hand and leading her along behind the old man's shuffle, "you're being pretty mean yourself, so we're even."

They were near the windows now, and ahead of her Lorraine could discern the outline of the stooped but still tall man. "Mr. Brandt," she said, "where are you taking me?"

His pause was brief. "This sidewalk cafe. I thought we might rest a moment and watch the boats on the river."

"Boats?" Lorraine heard the scrape of a chair.

"My dear," Brandt said, and he took hold of the arm that Tess had released. "Please."

Lorraine felt for the chair and eased herself into it. She could hear the squeaking of Tess's sneakers as the girl whispered into her patient's ear, "Have fun!" then turned toward other voices in the room.

"Boats?" Lorraine asked again. "What river? There's no river—"

"Oh, yes, there is. The Seine, of course. Hear it?" Brandt asked.

"I hear rain," Lorraine scoffed. "Just rain."

She could feel the heat of his body as he leaned toward her. "Just rain, Lorraine? Listen." She felt his fingers brush her shoulder as his arm went across the back of her chair.

"All right," the old woman said. "I'm listening, and I hear you calling me by my first name."

He lowered his voice both in pitch and volume. "Oui, chérie. C'ést Lorraine, non?" He took his arm from behind her, and she felt him reach across the table. She recognized the sound of ice in a water pitcher, and as she squinted, she could identify four glasses. He pulled two of the thick plastic glasses toward them, turned them right-side-up, then reached for the pitcher. "Bien!" he said. "Le garçon has brought us the vino."

"Oh, for heaven's sake," Lorraine said, straightening in her chair.

"And such beautiful goblets," he continued. "Waterford crystal, I'm sure." Brandt flicked the side of one of the water glasses with his fingernail, and Lorraine heard a dull thuck. He poured a small amount of water into one glass, set the pitcher down, brought the glass to his lips, and sipped. "Bravo!" he said, and Lorraine watched through her usual haze as he raised his other hand, kissed his fingertips, and said again, "Bien!"

She scooted forward to watch him fill the second glass. Then he reached for her hand, turned it over, and placed the glass in it. He leaned toward her. "What's French for 'to your health'?" he whispered.

"Ha!" she snorted. "It's a little late for that, you old fool."

"Jamais!" he said, then added, "That does mean 'never,' doesn't it?"

Lorraine couldn't help smiling. "Mr. Brandt—"

"Carl."

"Well, Mr. Carl—" and she shrugged and lifted her glass. "À tu."

She heard snickering from behind her, undoubtedly Mr. Larinski and Mrs. Sougher, if not also Mr. Linkous. But it didn't matter. She took a long drink of her water, set the tumbler down, and said, "Oui. Trés bien."

Lorraine felt the old man's arm come around her chair again. She leaned back even further, and the warmth of that arm felt good on her aching shoulders. She felt for the glass and wrapped her fingers around it.

"Mr. Brandt."

"Carl," he insisted.

"Carl," she conceded. "Do you like the poetry of Victor Hugo?"

He hesitated, then said, "I don't believe I've had the pleasure. But I have certainly enjoyed Quasimodo. Could you recite a poem for me—in English?"

Smiling, she peered at him. His eyes seemed to be deep brown, perhaps a cataract in the left one. "No," she admitted, "but I have a copy of his collected works in my room––in English."

"Trés Bien!" he said once more. "Mañana."

"That's Spanish," she chuckled.

"It still means tomorrow," he said.

Lorraine straightened, her upper body now turned toward Carl. She lifted her glass and tipped it so that he could drink from it. She waited for him to swallow and lick his lips, then cocked her head and smiled wider. "You know, I think I hear Maurice Chevalier singing."

"You're right!" Carl turned toward the windows. "Look! He's coming down the street. And Gigi is with him."

Lorraine looked where he was pointing, looked hard, and

sure enough, there beyond the rain-streaked window was the Seine. A man in a straw hat was coming toward them, a young girl on his arm. In the distance Lorraine could just make out the Champs Elysses and the Tuileries and the Louvre and the rose window of the cathedral and, in the far, far distance, Fontainbleau.

"Oh, Carl," she sighed as she patted the old man's gnarled hand, "Trés bien. Trés Bien."

HOUSE UPON THE SAND
by Carol Van Meter

With a ping, the bullet from the old battered twenty-two hit the solid metal blade of the oncoming bulldozer barely visible in the early morning fog. A lifetime of peace was smashed now, flattened like that bit of lead. Martha waited, hidden behind a rock wall in her narrow mountain valley, the home she'd come to as a young bride, fifty-one years ago.

"Please stop. Please don't make me do this awful thing." She thought. Uncaring, the machine plodded toward the rusty rabbit-wire fence that surrounded her vegetable garden. Under its heavy weight, the slender steel threads stretched to the ground, then snapped back to curl around a teetering fence post. With trembling fingers, Martha wiped her pale, watery, blue eyes and sighted carefully along the rifle, then she squeezed. Pop! The bullet exploded the right front headlight, and the driver hesitated as if trying to determine the cause of the breaking glass. The dozer rolled to a stop just inside her property.

Cocking his head sideways, favoring one ear, the driver leaned forward, alert to the slightest movement. Martha eased her thin body, still strong from hard work and healthy food, back down behind the wall. "Kid," the driver from the

Kingston Mining Company yelled, "you'd better stop this right now, or I'm gonna bust your butt!"

They'd sent her a bunch of letters that she'd hardly glanced at before she'd thrown them away. All their whereases and therefores about how, under the terms of Kentucky's broad-form deed law, they could strip mine her land didn't mean a thing because she'd been so certain she owned her land totally. James would've made sure of that. Her wonderful husband wouldn't have died and left her unprotected like this. Yesterday she'd found her deed—no mineral rights.

Martha heard the bulldozer engine rev up and the gears lock into place. The ground shook as it rumbled toward her. Bullets—someone else's—splattered off the dozer. Martha peeked over the wall to see the driver scramble to the ground. The driverless machine, now in reverse, backed slowly away.

Martha ran for her house. "Wilbur!" she exclaimed as her dear friend came lumbering, in an old man's bent-knee gait, out from behind a tree, "you saved my life."

A broad smile wrinkled his sixty-eight-year-old face. Straightening to his full height and expanding his chest, he grinned. "That's what us superheroes are for." Basking in Martha's admiration, he ushered her through the back door of her house. "Let's go sit on the front porch. We don't want to miss the action."

Martha and Wilbur sat in a wicker swing so they could get a full view of the action in the creek where the bulldozer was lying upside down with its treads still grinding away like a turtle on its back.

In half an hour, the excitement at the creek bank had shriveled to the laborious process of dragging the heavy bulldozer back up to the road. The sheriff ambled along Martha's walk and up her steps. The obviously strong man with straight black hair and wide cheek bones, a throw back to the time when this had been Cherokee territory, stopped before actually setting foot on the green-painted wooden porch. He leaned casually against a post, waiting to be invited to come closer.

"Mornin', Aunt Martha...Wilbur." He removed his uniform hat in a gesture of respect to the lady.

"Nice to see you, Dave," Martha said. "Won't you come on in and sit a spell."

"What's all the excitement over at the creek, Davie?" Wilbur asked, obviously trying hard to act casual.

Dave stared knowingly at the couple in the swing. "I'd imagine that you two know a lot more about what's going on than I do."

"What makes you say that?" Martha asked.

The sheriff ran his hand through his hair in an automatic movement that erased the indention caused by his hatband. "Well," he flipped the little gold tassels on his hat and watched them dangle back and forth, "those boys out there may be outsiders, but they'll eventually figure out who wanted to stop them."

"I thought I heard them yelling at a young boy." Wilbur commented, barely able to contain his excitement.

"An old fool would be more like it." The sheriff looked straight at the older man. "Wilbur, if you don't look like the cat who caught the canary, I don't know who does."

Wilbur's face broke into a grin. All thoughts of secrecy were overridden by the thrill of the story. "Davie, you should've been here. Martha was pinned down behind the wall with that driver, you know, that tub of lard named Harley. Anyway, that Harley feller was ready to run over her any second, and I come out a blastin'."

"Aunt Martha! You weren't in on this too!"

A smile tugged at her lips. Like Wilbur she was glad, proud of herself for standing up to those strip miners.

"I can't believe it, Aunt Martha. You could've been killed. I would've expected such foolishness from this...this," flustered, Dave gestured with his hand toward Wilbur, "...this old reprobate, but not you."

Wilbur stopped the swing abruptly. "What do you mean, old reprobate?"

Martha ignored Wilbur's outburst. "Dave, honey, I had to do something. They were gonna tear my house down."

"But Martha, the time to do something was ages ago. I know you knew what was happening, because I came here and talked to you about it myself."

"You did, Dave, but I was sure that when I found my deed, it would prove I owned my mineral rights. Unfortunately, like the foolish man in the Bible, my house was built on sand."

"What a mess." The sheriff expelled his breath tiredly.

"Dave, can't you get them to wait a little longer until I call my granddaughter, Susan. She's a lawyer. I know I should've called her sooner, but I didn't want to bother her."

The sheriff stood up and methodically placed his hat back on. "I'll see what I can do. But in the meantime," Dave poked his finger at Wilbur, "don't you even so much as frown at them. Right now they don't have any idea who took those potshots. Let's keep it that way."

Shortly after Dave left, Martha watched Wilbur walk down the path toward his house before she went into the kitchen to clean up. He was such a good friend. Since James had died, and before, he'd made almost all the repairs on this house. Actually, he'd built more of it than James had. James had had more important things to do. He'd been such a scholar. People said he was the best English teacher who had ever taught at Turkey Creek High School.

The clatter of a diesel engine interrupted Martha's memories. She dropped her dishtowel and hurried to the front porch. The first dozer was still in the creek, but Harley was in another one and heading right toward her property. Without giving any thought to what she was letting herself in for, she ran for her rifle. Back outside, she lifted the gun, steadied it and aimed for the engine. As soon as the front of the machine crossed onto her land, she squeezed the trigger three times in succession, and the big machine sputtered, chugged, wheezed, and then stopped.

•••

Straightening his tie for the fiftieth time, Wilbur followed Martha and Susan up the court house steps. He eyed the black-suited lawyers getting out of a long limousine.

"Susan, you watch out for those Kingston fellers. They're slick."

Laughing, Susan, with blonde hair and blue eyes that clearly distinguished truth from fiction, turned to pat Wilbur reassuringly on the shoulder. "Today in court, we will only be asking for a temporary injunction to stop Kingston Mining so that we can have time to prepare our case. There's no doubt in my mind that the judge will grant our request. John is extremely fair."

Back at Martha's after the hearing, the two women sat at the kitchen table, each with an untouched cup of coffee in her hands. Susan tried to explain to Martha just how precarious her position was. "Grandma, you are up against a powerful company. When a lot of money is at stake, people can get very nasty. You did damage their equipment."

"Honey, use your head. Suppose Kingston does bring

charges. Who would arrest me? Not Dave. He was in my Sunday school class when he was a boy. Can you see him, or any of his deputies, dragging me off to jail? And who would issue the order, the judge? John was your best friend in high school."

Before Susan could answer, the telephone rang. She picked it up. After a lengthy conversation in which she did most of the listening, She walked over to Martha and gave her a hug to ease the bad news. "Grandma, Dave just called to say that Kingston tried to file charges for attempted murder against you, but John talked him out of it." Martha gasped. "He says not to worry. Kingston was just trying to scare you."

"He did," Martha said as she shakily set her cup down and stood up. "I think I'll go to my room and lie down for a while."

It was all Martha could do to conceal her trembling hands until she reached her bedroom. Everything had gotten out of hand, moved too fast. She swayed and nearly lost her balance before she sat heavily on her bed, and then fell back against her pillow. This is crazy, she thought. The shot hadn't gone close to Harley. Her breath grew short and fast. She felt as if her whole body was about to explode. What was she going to do?

She picked up the phone and dialed Wilbur's number. When he answered, she told him about the attempted murder charge.

"Martha!" Wilbur answered. "If you don't lead the most exciting life. I'll get my car and be right over. We'll pick us up a couple of Tommy guns and head out just like Bonnie and Clyde. We'll go blastin' and robbin' our way to Canada. On second thought, we'd better head for Mexico. Cold weather makes my arthritis worse."

His reaction was so unexpected Martha started laughing. "Wilbur! This is serious." As her laughs settled down, she said, "What am I going to do with you?"

"You could," his voice grew serious, "let me help you through a bad time."

"You always do." She pulled the pillow more comfortably under her head. "At the worst times in my life you've been able to help me smile."

Wilbur let out a long tired breath. "That's me, Martha, a laugh a minute."

•••

For the next three weeks, Susan, with the help of her friends, launched a state-wide publicity campaign to help get a law passed in the state legislature that would repeal the broad form deed. Their efforts were rewarded with growing support for the bill.

As the two women sat on the front porch one evening, watching the twilight turn to darkness, Wilbur came up the steps and sat down beside Susan on the swing.

"Wilbur, where have you been hiding yourself?"

"Oh, I've been busy," Wilbur replied.

"Ha, you just don't want to help us," Martha teased.

Wilbur shook his head vigorously. "It's not that, Martha. I swear it's not. I just don't like being in the house with all those women, their legs propped up and everything showing, almost."

"Wilbur, you old coot," Martha said, "you're too old for it to make any difference to you."

Hurt, Wilbur replied indignantly, "Maybe so, but I've got a good memory." For the next few minutes no one said anything. But one look at Wilbur's crossed arms and grouchy expression and Susan, or Martha, would start to laugh. After enduring their sporadic giggles as long as he could, Wilbur finally asked, "What did you want me to stop by here for, Martha? I don't have all night."

"Oh, yes. Wilbur dear...."

"It's 'Wilbur dear' now, is it? Not so long ago I was an 'old coot'."

"Don't be angry," Martha cajoled, "we weren't laughing at you."

Wilbur didn't say anything. He just shrugged his shoulders.

"Anyway," Martha continued, "I want you to do me a favor. Would you please plant those tomato plants? Just in case." She pointed to a half an egg carton with six plants much too big for the small root space. "You know, they're the ones James and I saved seeds from over the years."

"I don't see why you bother. 'Better Boys' are healthier and more blight resistant."

"But ours are bigger."

"Maybe, but the insides are tough and green. Skin splits easy, too."

Martha didn't say a word. She slowly got up and went inside.

"What's with her?" Wilbur asked.

"You know how important those tomatoes are to her," Susan snapped. "She loves them because she planted them with Grandpa."

"Oh blast, she's been moonin' over Jimmy too long. He never was half the man she thought he was anyway. Comes a time to let go and look at the real world."

Susan had never heard Wilbur say an unkind word about her grandmother. Why? As long as she could remember, even when her grandfather was living, Wilbur had been devoted to her grandmother, practically her slave. With new insight, Susan studied the dejected man in overalls and checked flannel shirt.

"Wilbur," Susan ventured, "are you in love with my grand-mother?"

For a few minutes he didn't say anything. He just stared out into the dark. Finally, Wilbur turned to Susan, rubbed an age-spotted hand over his thin hair and took a deep breath, letting it out slowly.

"I should've asked her first. I would've been a much better husband than Jimmy. He never could fix anything. If it hadn't been for Martha and me, this old house would've fallen down around her ears. And I loved her more, too."

Astounded, Susan could only stare. Then finally she said, "It isn't too late. You could still ask her."

"You heard her. I'm an old coot, no good for anything."

"Wilbur, she didn't mean it that way. She was only teasing." When Susan thought of all the years of desire and frustration he'd glossed over with humor, she almost wept. "Nothing is ever too late, until it's too late."

"Ha," he snorted as he slowly stood up, limping with the first pressure on his arthritic knee. "I'd better get these tomatoes in the ground." He picked up the plants and started down the steps.

Martha's cause continued to gain public support during the next few weeks. Susan and her friends staged one last event, a barbecue at Martha's on the evening before the big vote in the legislature. If the broad form deed was repealed, Susan was sure there would be too much pressure on the judge for him to rule against Martha.

As the party wound down, Wilbur searched for Martha. She wasn't in the pasture where the bonfire was finally dying down. He'd just come from there. He scanned the area on the other side of her house. Not for the first time, he wished he could see better at night. He spotted a lone figure on her knees and stooping over in the middle of her garden. What on earth? He hurried to her side.

"Martha, what are you doing out here?"

Head bent, she wept into her hands. Wilbur dropped down on his knees in front of her and took her in his arms.

"Oh, Wilbur," she choked out before the tears started rolling again. "Look." She held up a broken cabbage plant. "They walked all over my garden." She sniffed and he gave her his handkerchief. "They broke my tomato plants."

Wilbur held her tightly. "Don't worry, honey. I planted the ones you gave me, and they're safe and sound."

"It's not just that." Martha stopped to wipe her eyes. "Everything is so mixed up. I don't understand. These people are supposed to be my friends. Look." She pointed at the churned up earth. "Someone turned a car in my lettuce bed."

Wilbur pulled her toward him and cradled her head against his chest. "It's going to be all right. The potatoes and beans will be fine. They're still deep in the ground."

"But my tomatoes? James and my tomatoes."

Wilbur clamped her head tightly against him. "Martha, when are you going to look at Jimmy the way he was, instead of under that halo. Face facts. Jimmy wasn't half the man you thought he was, then or now. He was lazy."

Martha's head snapped up. "You stop...."

Wilbur went on, "For once in your life listen to the truth. Jimmy didn't do any more work around this place than he had to. You know that. Who did I see up on that roof all those times, spreading tar?"

"I just patched it once in a while."

"Don't try to kid me. Your old roof had so much tar on it that it looked like a polka dot umbrella. And who worked this garden? You and the kids."

"But James needed time alone to work on his poetry. He was a brillant man," Martha agreed.

"No he wasn't. Oh, I'll admit, Jimmy knew big words all right, but he used those over people."

Wilbur continued, "Worst of all, he put you down. Little by little, he took over your mind. When you were young, you had all the confidence in the world. The longer you were with Jimmy, the more you retreated into yourself. I saw it happening, but I couldn't do anything about it. You'd never listen to me. It wasn't until several years after he died that you started being yourself again. Jimmy had a nice cozy life, with you and the children waiting on him hand and foot. All of you were always trying to live up to the standards he set for you. You're still trying."

"What's wrong with having standards?"

"Nothing, if they're yours." Wilbur answered. "Let go, Martha. Don't keep yourself tied up in knots." His voice strained with quiet intensity. "Let yourself live the last of your life for you. For Martha Morrison, the smartest girl in school."

Martha stared up at his weathered face. He moved closer, the man she'd cared for longer than anyone, ever since grade school.

"Martha, I loved you then. I love you now."

His lips touched hers, hesitantly. She could move away if she wanted to. She rested her unpracticed hands on the sides of his waist. Then, as if her hands were making the decisions instead of her mind, they slid around to his back and held tight. It had been years since she'd been this close to anyone, held a man in this way. She pulled him closer. A rush of long forgotten emotion that she thought was impossible for her to experience after all this time, flashed through her body. Her heart raced. She held on for dear life.

A distant laugh floated to them, and they ended their kiss like guilty teenagers who'd been caught. Wilbur helped her up and walked her out of the garden. As they reached her front steps, Martha pulled her hand out of Wilbur's. She stepped up on the first step and turned to Wilbur and said, "I need to go in now."

"Yeah." Wilbur grinned, understanding Martha's inability to adapt to the change in their relationship. "I'm a little tired myself. I hope the legislature votes your way tomorrow."

"Me too. It's pretty much all or nothing. Susan has based everything on this vote."

"Are you worried?"

Martha looked down at him. "I should be, but somehow I'm not."

•••

Susan, and Martha's supporters, left very early the next morning for the State Capitol in Frankfort. After they were gone, Martha walked through her house, now quiet for the first time in weeks. She looked at the stacks of posters, boxes of paper and envelopes, and the other remnants of the media campaign. She also looked at the cracks in the ceiling, the uneven floors, mismatched doors, and out of date kitchen. Somehow, her home had lost its luster, as had her memories.

Late in the evening, the phone rang. Susan was on the line, her voice near tears, "Grandmother, I'm so sorry. They didn't even vote on our bill. They adjourned without bringing it to the floor."

Martha took a deep breath, then let it out slowly. "You tried really hard. Thank you."

"We're not finished by a long shot. I'll fly back to Phila-delphia in the morning, check up on a few matters at my office, and then I'll be back in a few days. We'll harass Kingston until he decides it's too much trouble to mine here."

Martha walked out into her backyard. She closed her eyes and tilted her face up, enjoying the heat of the last rays of the evening sun on her face. She took a deep breath. It felt good to be alive.

Today was a new beginning. No longer would she depend on others to take care of her. Wilbur was right, she had based her life on Jimmy's values, and on the well-meaning but un-dependable support of the community, and the legal system. It was time for a change.

Wilbur and Susan had been great supporters during times of trouble; but it wasn't fair for them to have to look after her. Martha straightened her shoulders. She could stand on her own two feet.

"Hey Martha, what are you doing out here?" Wilbur asked as he rounded the corner of her house.

"Thinking."

He pulled out a chair and sat down. "What about?"

"Life, friends." She paused then continued, "I guess you heard the legislature didn't pass the bill."

"Yeah. Susan called. She thought you might be upset."

Martha smiled. "No."

Wilbur smiled. "Good. All the fun's gone out of it any-way." He picked up her hand and squeezed it. "But we sure had them going that morning when they tried to cross your land, didn't we?"

The softly scented evening breeze carried dandelion-seed parachutes through the air.

Wilbur leaned forward. "Say listen, Martha. For a long

time now I've wanted to go on some of those tours to the Holy Lands, or Hawaii, maybe Australia. You know, those places they're always showing on TV." He picked up her hand and kissed her knuckles. "Since you won't be tied up here, why don't you go with me?"

Martha looked him straight in the eye, and smiled. "Wilbur, are you making an indecent proposition to me?"

"Lord, Martha, at my age it's hard to say, but I sure as hell hope so."

ABOUT THE AUTHORS

JESSE STUART
(The Slipover Sweater & Melungeon Marriage)

Jesse Stuart (1906-1984) was a famous Kentucky writer and teacher. He published more than 2000 poems, 460 short stories, and more than sixty books, which have immortalized the Kentucky hill country that inspired his writing.

ANCELLA R. BICKLEY
(Martha)

Ancella R. Bickley is a native of Huntington, West Virginia. She holds bachelor's and master's degrees in English from West Virginia State College and Marshall University, respectively, and a doctorate in education from West Virginia University. A retired teacher and college administrator, she has spent much of the last fifteen years researching the history of black people in West Virginia. She says that she began to write because the literature with which she was familiar

reflected few images of the kinds of black people that she has met in her home area. "They are wonderfully resourceful and resilient people who have struggled to build lives in Appalachia," she says, "and I want to tell their stories."

JAMES M. GIFFORD
(Missing in Action in Appalachia & James Alexander Moore)

James M. Gifford is the Executive Director of the Jesse Stuart Foundation, a not-for-profit regional press and bookseller. Dr. Gifford received the B.A. degree from Maryville College, the M.A. degree from Middle Tennessee State University, and his Ph.D. in history from the University of Georgia. He has published in historical, educational, and literary journals, and he has won professional awards as a teacher, author, editor, and publisher. "My story," he reflects, "is about the lost opportunities that affect every person's life."

JIMMY LOWE
(Ben Paxton's Heart)

Jimmy Lowe is a teacher and writer from Glasgow, Kentucky. Recently retired after 27 years as a high school English teacher, Lowe now teaches for Western Kentucky University and travels the state performing his one-man play, *Yours Respectfully, Jesse Stuart*. His interest in Stuart also led him to write the children's biography, *The Boy From Dark Hills*, which was published by the Jesse Stuart Foundation. Lowe's other writing includes the play, *Old Luther's Store*. His photography has appeared in national newspapers, magazines, books, and on television.

JAMES B. GOODE
(Buttons and Bows)

James B. Goode is Professor of English at the University of Kentucky Lexington Community College. James holds A.A., B.A., and M.A. degrees from the University of Kentucky and has done additional graduate work at the Universities of Detroit and Chicago. His major published books include *Appalachian Mountain Mother* (1969), *The Whistle and the Wind* (1971), *Poets of Darkness* (1981), *Up From The Mines* (1993), *Ancient Sunshine: The Story of Coal* (1997), and *The Cutting Edge: Mining in the Twenty-First Century* (due for release in 2001). His documentary films include "Lynch: A Coal Legacy" and "Coal, Steel, Machines, & Men: The Benham Story." He has published over 500 poems in national and international magazines, and written over two hundred newspaper columns.

EDWINA PENDARVIS
(Roses So Red)

Edwina Pendarvis lives in Huntington, West Virginia, where she teaches at Marshall University. Born in eastern Kentucky, she often writes about people and places there. Her poems and essays appear in regional journals such as *Antietam Review*, *Appalachian Journal*, *Now and Then*, and *Wind Magazine*; and a collection of her poetry is featured in *Human Landscapes* by Bottom Dog Press. She has written introductions to three Jesse Stuart Foundation collections of poetry: Jesse Stuart's *Harvest Of Youth*, Rebecca Bailey's *A Wild Kentucky Garden*, and Billy C. Clark's *To Leave My Heart at Catlettsburg*.

LAURA TREACY BENTLEY
(The Legend of Aracoma)

Laura Treacy Bentley is a poet from Huntington, West Virginia who teaches gifted students in Cabell County and moonlights frequently at Marshall University. Her work appeared in *Poetry Ireland Review, The Stinging Fly* (Ireland), *Antietam Review, Eureka Literary Magazine, Art Times,* among others, and in five anthologies. She won a Fellowship Award for Literature from the WV Commission on the Arts in 1994 and has written a novella entitled *Water Street.* Work is forthcoming in *ELM* and *Now and Then.* She recently completed a four-week writing residency in County Clare, Ireland and read in Dublin at the Irish Writers' Centre in June of 2000. Her first collection of poetry, *In The Untangling,* will be published in Ireland by Salmon Publishing.

BRUCE RADFORD RICHEY
(Old Pap's Story)

Bruce Radford Richey, a native of Monroe County, Kentucky, traveled the United States for 31 years as a Defense Department Inspector. Now retired, he recently moved from Frankfort to Ashland to devote more time and energy to volunteer work at the Jesse Stuart Nature Preserve. In addition to his government work, he has owned and operated a restaurant and worked in the music industry. If it's broke, Bruce can fix it!

INA EVERMAN
(Helpful Romantics)

Ina Everman lives in Independence, Kentucky, and has taught at Twenhofel Middle School for 26 years. She is an avid reader and a firm supporter of the Jesse Stuart Foundation, teaching a unit of Kentucky literature and directing a Jesse Stuart Literary Society for her eighth graders. This is only her second published short story, but several poems have been included in anthologies. She hopes to publish a book of stories and poems in the near future.

DANNY FULKS
(First String)

Danny Fulks grew up on a farm in southern Ohio where his parents worked the land and milked cows. He earned a doctorate in education from the University of Tennessee at Knoxville. His nonfiction and personal essays have appeared in *The MacGuffin*, *Goldenseal*, *Timeline*, *Now And Then*, *Hearthstone*, and *In Buckeye Country*. A collection of his work, *Tales Along The Appalachian Plateau*, was published in 1995 by Bottom Dog Press. A tri-state area that includes Ohio, Kentucky, and West Virginia provides the setting for most of Mr. Fulk's work. His topics include food, humor, murder, sports, music, moonshine, Mail Pouch barns, cave exploration, religion, and the Ohio River. He lives in Huntington, WV.

LOYAL JONES
(Laura)

Loyal Jones, a native of Cherokee County, North Carolina, grew up on a mountain farm. He studied at Berea College and the University of North Carolina at Chapel Hill. He recently retired from his long-time position as Director of the Appalachian Center at Berea College, where he taught Appalachian Studies courses and organized annual celebrations of regional culture. Jones is widely published on Appalachian life, values, religion, humor, and music.

BILLY C. CLARK
(The Fiddle and the Fruit Jar)

Billy C. Clark, "the chronicler of the Big Sandy region," writes about the unique river culture of southern Appalachia. Today this native of Catlettsburg, Kentucky lives in Farmville, Virginia and edits *Virginia Writing*, an award-winning publication which features the writing and art of high school students.

LINDA SCOTT DEROSIER
(Branch Dance)

Linda Scott DeRosier was born in the upper room of her grandmother's log house at Boone's Camp, Kentucky. She received her BS degree from Pikeville College at age twenty and went on to complete a cross-disciplinary doctorate (Ph.D.) in philosophy, education and psychology at the University of Kentucky. She holds a master's degree from Eastern Kentucky University and one from Harvard. She is the 1999 recipient of the Frances Shaw Writing Fellowship granted by the Ragdale Foundation, Lake Forest, Illinois, where she spent June and July in residency working on a novel. She is the author of *Creeker: A Woman's Journey.*

CHRISTINA ST. CLAIR
(Connected)

Christina St. Clair is a seeker of meaning and authenticity. This led her to bum around Europe long before it was fashionable. She then moved from England to the U.S. where she did many jobs and ended up a non-degreed chemist. She has two patents in analytical chemistry. She is currently working on a degree in philosophy and is also receiving training in spiritual direction at West Virginia Spiritual Institute. She began writing in 1986 and is now a full time writer and hopes that her work will resonate at many levels, especially the transcendental.

ALEXANDRA COMBS HUDSON
(A Matter of Perspective)

Alexandra Hudson was born in Eastern Kentucky, and returned there after attending the University of Kentucky School of Journalism in the early seventies. She has spent 25 years in business management in home medical equipment, medical and commercial gases, welding supplies and equipment. She has had several articles published in *The Troublesome Creek Times*, and one in *Mountain Magazine*. "A Matter of Perspective" is her first published short story.

KATE LARKEN
(Evelyn Alice was a Farm Woman)

Kate Larken, ad hoc activist and co-writer/director of Two Many Hats Company's touring play, "Teddy's Place," is a former journalist, trainer of horses and pumper of petrol who, for a time, also made her living as a professional musician, songwriter, storyteller and actor. She now writes and works as a kid wrangler (schoolteacher) in her native Kentucky.

Barbara Smith
(On the Left Bank)

Barbara Smith, free-lance writer and editor and medical ethicist, is Emerita Professor of Literature and Writing and Chair of the Division of the Humanities at Alderson-Broaddus College in Philippi, West Virginia. She has published over three hundred poems, short stories and journal articles, plus a novel (*Six Miles Out*) and seven books of nonfiction and served as contributing editor for three poetry anthologies. Two new books of her fiction are awaiting publication.

Carol Van Meter
(House Upon the Sand)

In her novel, *House Upon The Sand,* from which this story is taken, Carol Van Meter draws from her Eastern Kentucky heritage, rich in language and characters. In the novel, Martha believes the local judge and sheriff will protect her from the outsiders who want to strip mine her land. She struggles to come to terms with the erosion of that support.

Along with writing, Van Meter trades stocks and stock options. When asked why she does such two diverse activities at the same time, she answered, "Writing lets me glance occasionally at my quotation screen while keeping me from making a trade because I'm bored." She lives with her husband, Greg, in Huntington, West Virginia.